Malbone: An Oldport Romance

by Thomas Wentworth Higginson

PRELUDE.

AS one wanders along this southwestern promontory of the Isle of Peace, and looks down upon the green translucent water which forever bathes the marble slopes of the Pirates' Cave, it is natural to think of the ten wrecks with which the past winter has strewn this shore. Though almost all trace of their presence is already gone, yet their mere memory lends to these cliffs a human interest. Where a stranded vessel lies, thither all steps converge, so long as one plank remains upon another. There centres the emotion. All else is but the setting, and the eye sweeps with indifference the line of unpeopled rocks. They are barren, till the imagination has tenanted them with possibilities of danger and dismay. The ocean provides the scenery and properties of a perpetual tragedy, but the interest arrives with the performers. Till then the shores remain vacant, like the great conventional armchairs of the French drama, that wait for Rachel to come and die.

Yet as I ride along this fashionable avenue in August, and watch the procession of the young and fair,—as I look at stately houses, from each of which has gone forth almost within my memory a funeral or a bride,—then every thoroughfare of human life becomes in fancy but an ocean shore, with its ripples and its wrecks. One learns, in growing older, that no fiction can be so strange nor appear so improbable as would the simple truth; and that doubtless even Shakespeare did but timidly transcribe a few of the deeds and passions he had personally known. For no man of middle age can dare trust himself to portray life in its full intensity, as he has studied or shared it; he must resolutely set aside as indescribable the things most worth describing, and must expect to be charged with exaggeration, even when he tells the rest.

I. AN ARRIVAL.

IT was one of the changing days of our Oldport midsummer. In the morning it had rained in rather a dismal way, and Aunt Jane had said she should put it in her diary. It was a very serious thing for the elements when they got into Aunt Jane's diary. By noon the sun came out as clear and sultry as if there had never been a cloud, the northeast wind died away, the bay was motionless, the first locust of the summer shrilled from the elms, and the robins seemed to be serving up butterflies hot for their insatiable second brood, while nothing seemed desirable for a human luncheon except ice-cream and fans. In the afternoon the southwest wind came up the bay, with its line of dark-blue ripple and its delicious coolness; while the hue of the water grew more and more intense, till we seemed to be living in the heart of a sapphire.

The household sat beneath the large western doorway of the old Maxwell House,—he rear door, which looks on the water. The house had just been reoccupied by my Aunt Jane, whose great-grandfather had built it, though it had for several generations been out of the family. I know no finer specimen of those

3

large colonial dwellings in which the genius of Sir Christopher Wren bequeathed traditions of stateliness to our democratic days. Its central hall has a carved archway; most of the rooms have painted tiles and are wainscoted to the ceiling; the sashes are red-cedar, the great staircase mahogany; there are pilasters with delicate Corinthian capitals; there are cherubs' heads and wings that go astray and lose themselves in closets and behind glass doors; there are curling acanthus-leaves that cluster over shelves and ledges, and there are those graceful shell-patterns which one often sees on old furniture, but rarely in houses. The high front door still retains its Ionic cornice; and the western entrance, looking on the bay, is surmounted by carved fruit and flowers, and is crowned, as is the roof, with that pineapple in whose symbolic wealth the rich merchants of the last century delighted.

Like most of the statelier houses in that region of Oldport, this abode had its rumors of a ghost and of secret chambers. The ghost had never been properly lionized nor laid, for Aunt Jane, the neatest of housekeepers, had discouraged all silly explorations, had at once required all barred windows to be opened, all superfluous partitions to be taken down, and several highly eligible dark-closets to be nailed up. If there was anything she hated, it was nooks and odd corners. Yet there had been times that year, when the household would have been glad to find a few more such hiding-places; for during the first few weeks the house had been crammed with guests so closely that the very mice had been ill-accommodated and obliged to sit up all night, which had caused them much discomfort and many audible disagreements.

But this first tumult had passed away; and now there remained only the various nephews and nieces of the house, including a due proportion of small children. Two final guests were to arrive that day, bringing the latest breath of Europe on their wings,—Philip Malbone, Hope's betrothed; and little Emilia, Hope's half-sister.

None of the family had seen Emilia since her wandering mother had taken her abroad, a fascinating spoiled child of four, and they were all eager to see in how many ways the succeeding twelve years had completed or corrected the spoiling. As for Philip, he had been spoiled, as Aunt Jane declared, from the day of his birth, by the joint effort of all friends and neighbors. Everybody had conspired to carry on the process except Aunt Jane herself, who directed toward him one of her honest, steady, immovable dislikes, which may be said to have dated back to the time when his father and mother were married, some years before he personally entered on the scene.

The New York steamer, detained by the heavy fog of the night before, now came in unwonted daylight up the bay. At the first glimpse, Harry and the boys pushed off in the row-boat; for, as one of the children said, anybody who had been to Venice would naturally wish to come to the very house in a gondola. In another half-hour there was a great entanglement of embraces at the water-side, for the guests had landed.

Malbone's self-poised easy grace was the same as ever; his chestnut-brown eyes were as winning, his features as handsome; his complexion, too clearly pink for a man, had a sea bronze upon it: he was the same Philip who had left

4

home, though with some added lines of care. But in the brilliant little fairy beside him all looked in vain for the Emilia they remembered as a child. Her eyes were more beautiful than ever,—the darkest violet eyes, that grew luminous with thought and almost black with sorrow. Her gypsy taste, as everybody used to call it, still showed itself in the scarlet and dark blue of her dress; but the clouded gypsy tint had gone from her cheek, and in its place shone a deep carnation, so hard and brilliant that it appeared to be enamelled on the surface, yet so firm and deep-dyed that it seemed as if not even death could ever blanch it. There is a kind of beauty that seems made to be painted on ivory, and such was hers. Only the microscopic pencil of a miniature-painter could portray those slender eyebrows, that arched caressingly over the beautiful eyes,—or the silky hair of darkest chestnut that crept in a wavy line along the temples, as if longing to meet the brows,—or those unequalled lashes! "Unnecessarily long," Aunt Jane afterwards pronounced them; while Kate had to admit that they did indeed give Emilia an overdressed look at breakfast, and that she ought to have a less showy set to match her morning costume.

But what was most irresistible about Emilia,—that which we all noticed in this interview, and which haunted us all thenceforward,—was a certain wild, entangled look she wore, as of some untamed out-door thing, and a kind of pathetic lost sweetness in her voice, which made her at once and forever a heroine of romance with the children. Yet she scarcely seemed to heed their existence, and only submitted to the kisses of Hope and Kate as if that were a part of the price of coming home, and she must pay it.

Had she been alone, there might have been an awkward pause; for if you expect a cousin, and there alights a butterfly of the tropics, what hospitality can you offer? But no sense of embarrassment ever came near Malbone, especially with the children to swarm over him and claim him for their own. Moreover, little Helen got in the first remark in the way of serious conversation.

"Let me tell him something!" said the child. "Philip! that doll of mine that you used to know, only think! she was sick and died last summer, and went into the rag-bag. And the other split down the back, so there was an end of her."

Polar ice would have been thawed by this reopening of communication. Philip soon had the little maid on his shoulder,—the natural throne of all children,—and they went in together to greet Aunt Jane.

Aunt Jane was the head of the house,—a lady who had spent more than fifty years in educating her brains and battling with her ailments. She had received from her parents a considerable inheritance in the way of whims, and had nursed it up into a handsome fortune. Being one of the most impulsive of human beings, she was naturally one of the most entertaining; and behind all her eccentricities there was a fund of the soundest sense and the tenderest affection. She had seen much and varied society, had been greatly admired in her youth, but had chosen to remain unmarried. Obliged by her physical condition to make herself the first object, she was saved from utter selfishness by sympathies as democratic as her personal habits were exclusive. Unexpected and commonly fantastic in her doings, often dismayed by small difficulties, but never by large

5

ones, she sagaciously administered the affairs of all those around her,—planned their dinners and their marriages, fought out their bargains and their feuds.

She hated everything irresolute or vague; people might play at cat's-cradle or study Spinoza, just as they pleased; but, whatever they did, they must give their minds to it. She kept house from an easy-chair, and ruled her dependants with severity tempered by wit, and by the very sweetest voice in which reproof was ever uttered. She never praised them, but if they did anything particularly well, rebuked them retrospectively, asking why they had never done it well before? But she treated them munificently, made all manner of plans for their comfort, and they all thought her the wisest and wittiest of the human race. So did the youths and maidens of her large circle; they all came to see her, and she counselled, admired, scolded, and petted them all. She had the gayest spirits, and an unerring eye for the ludicrous, and she spoke her mind with absolute plainness to all comers. Her intuitions were instantaneous as lightning, and, like that, struck very often in the wrong place. She was thus extremely unreasonable and altogether charming.

Such was the lady whom Emilia and Malbone went up to greet,—the one shyly, the other with an easy assurance, such as she always disliked. Emilia submitted to another kiss, while Philip pressed Aunt Jane's hand, as he pressed all women's, and they sat down.

"Now begin to tell your adventures," said Kate. "People always tell their adventures till tea is ready."

"Who can have any adventures left," said Philip, "after such letters as I wrote you all?"

"Of which we got precisely one!" said Kate. "That made it such an event, after we had wondered in what part of the globe you might be looking for the post-office! It was like finding a letter in a bottle, or disentangling a person from the Dark Ages."

"I was at Neuchatel two months; but I had no adventures. I lodged with a good Pasteur, who taught me geology and German."

"That is suspicious," said Kate. "Had he a daughter passing fair?"

"Indeed he had."

"And you taught her English? That is what these beguiling youths always do in novels."

"Yes."

"What was her name?"

"Lili."

"What a pretty name! How old was she?"

"She was six."

"O Philip!" cried Kate; "but I might have known it. Did she love you very much?"

Hope looked up, her eyes full of mild reproach at the possibility of doubting any child's love for Philip. He had been her betrothed for more than a year, during which time she had habitually seen him wooing every child he had met as if it were a woman,—which, for Philip, was saying a great deal. Happily they had in common the one trait of perfect amiability, and she knew no more how to be jealous than he to be constant.

"Lili was easily won," he said. "Other things being equal, people of six prefer that man who is tallest."

"Philip is not so very tall," said the eldest of the boys, who was listening eagerly, and growing rapidly.

"No," said Philip, meekly. "But then the Pasteur was short, and his brother was a dwarf."

"When Lili found that she could reach the ceiling from Mr. Malbone's shoulder," said Emilia, "she asked no more."

"Then you knew the pastor's family also, my child," said Aunt Jane, looking at her kindly and a little keenly.

"I was allowed to go there sometimes," she began, timidly.

"To meet her American Cousin," interrupted Philip. "I got some relaxation in the rules of the school. But, Aunt Jane, you have told us nothing about your health."

"There is nothing to tell," she answered. "I should like, if it were convenient, to be a little better. But in this life, if one can walk across the floor, and not be an idiot, it is something. That is all I aim at."

"Isn't it rather tiresome?" said Emilia, as the elder lady happened to look at her.

"Not at all," said Aunt Jane, composedly. "I naturally fall back into happiness, when left to myself."

"So you have returned to the house of your fathers," said Philip. "I hope you like it."

"It is commonplace in one respect," said Aunt Jane. "General Washington once slept here."

"Oh!" said Philip. "It is one of that class of houses?"

"Yes," said she. "There is not a village in America that has not half a dozen of them, not counting those where he only breakfasted. Did ever man sleep like that man? What else could he ever have done? Who governed, I wonder, while he was asleep? How he must have travelled! The swiftest horse could scarcely have carried him from one of these houses to another."

"I never was attached to the memory of Washington," meditated Philip; "but I always thought it was the pear-tree. It must have been that he was such a very unsettled person."

"He certainly was not what is called a domestic character," said Aunt Jane.

"I suppose you are, Miss Maxwell," said Philip. "Do you often go out?"

"Sometimes, to drive," said Aunt Jane. "Yesterday I went shopping with Kate, and sat in the carriage while she bought under-sleeves enough for a centipede. It is always so with that child. People talk about the trouble of getting a daughter ready to be married; but it is like being married once a month to live with her."

"I wonder that you take her to drive with you," suggested Philip, sympathetically.

"It is a great deal worse to drive without her," said the impetuous lady. "She is the only person who lets me enjoy things, and now I cannot enjoy them in her absence. Yesterday I drove alone over the three beaches, and left her at home with a dress-maker. Never did I see so many lines of surf; but they only seemed to me like some of Kate's ball-dresses, with the prevailing flounces, six deep. I was so enraged that she was not there, I wished to cover my face with my handkerchief. By the third beach I was ready for the madhouse."

"Is Oldport a pleasant place to live in?" asked Emilia, eagerly.

"It is amusing in the summer," said Aunt Jane, "though the society is nothing but a pack of visiting-cards. In winter it is too dull for young people, and only suits quiet old women like me, who merely live here to keep the Ten Commandments and darn their stockings."

Meantime the children were aiming at Emilia, whose butterfly looks amazed and charmed them, but who evidently did not know what to do with their eager affection.

"I know about you," said little Helen; "I know what you said when you were little."

"Did I say anything?" asked Emilia, carelessly.

"Yes," replied the child, and began to repeat the oft-told domestic tradition in an accurate way, as if it were a school lesson. "Once you had been naughty, and your papa thought it his duty to slap you, and you cried; and he told you in French, because he always spoke French with you, that he did not punish you for his own pleasure. Then you stopped crying, and asked, 'Pour le plaisir de qui alors?' That means 'For whose pleasure then?' Hope said it was a droll question for a little girl to ask."

"I do not think it was Emilia who asked that remarkable question, little girl," said Kate.

"I dare say it was," said Emilia; "I have been asking it all my life." Her eyes grew very moist, what with fatigue and excitement. But just then, as is apt to happen in this world, they were all suddenly recalled from tears to tea, and the children smothered their curiosity in strawberries and cream.

They sat again beside the western door, after tea. The young moon came from a cloud and dropped a broad path of glory upon the bay; a black yacht glided noiselessly in, and anchored amid this tract of splendor. The shadow of its masts was on the luminous surface, while their reflection lay at a different angle, and seemed to penetrate far below. Then the departing steamer went flashing across this bright realm with gorgeous lustre; its red and green lights were doubled in the paler waves, its four reflected chimneys chased each other among the reflected masts. This jewelled wonder passing, a single fishing-boat drifted silently by, with its one dark sail; and then the moon and the anchored yacht were left alone.

Presently some of the luggage came from the wharf. Malbone brought out presents for everybody; then all the family went to Europe in photographs, and with some reluctance came back to America for bed.

II. PLACE AUX DAMES!

IN every town there is one young maiden who is the universal favorite, who belongs to all sets and is made an exception to all family feuds, who is the confidante of all girls and the adopted sister of all young men, up to the time when they respectively offer themselves to her, and again after they are rejected. This post was filled in Oldport, in those days, by my cousin Kate.

Born into the world with many other gifts, this last and least definable gift of popularity was added to complete them all. Nobody criticised her, nobody was jealous of her, her very rivals lent her their new music and their lovers; and her own discarded wooers always sought her to be a bridesmaid when they married somebody else.

She was one of those persons who seem to have come into the world well-dressed. There was an atmosphere of elegance around her, like a costume; every attitude implied a presence-chamber or a ball-room. The girls complained that in private theatricals no combination of disguises could reduce Kate to the ranks, nor give her the "make-up" of a waiting-maid. Yet as her father was a New York merchant of the precarious or spasmodic description, she had been used from childhood to the wildest fluctuations of wardrobe;—a year of Paris dresses,—then another year spent in making over ancient finery, that never looked like either finery or antiquity when it came from her magic hands. Without a particle of vanity or fear, secure in health and good-nature and invariable prettiness, she cared little whether the appointed means of grace were ancient silk or modern muslin. In her periods of poverty, she made no secret of the necessary devices; the other girls, of course, guessed them, but her lovers never did, because she always told them. There was one particular tarlatan dress of hers which was a sort of local institution. It was known to all her companions, like the State House. There was a report that she had first worn it at her christening; the report originated with herself. The young men knew that she was going to the party if she could turn that pink tarlatan once more; but they had only the vaguest impression what a tarlatan was, and cared little on which side it was worn, so long as Kate was inside.

During these epochs of privation her life, in respect to dress, was a perpetual Christmas-tree of second-hand gifts. Wealthy aunts supplied her with cast-off shoes of all sizes, from two and a half up to five, and she used them all. She was reported to have worn one straw hat through five changes of fashion. It was averred that, when square crowns were in vogue, she flattened it over a tin pan, and that, when round crowns returned, she bent it on the bedpost. There was such a charm in her way of adapting these treasures, that the other girls liked to test her with new problems in the way of millinery and dress-making; millionnaire friends implored her to trim their hats, and lent her their own things in order to learn how to wear them. This applied especially to certain rich cousins, shy and studious girls, who adored her, and to whom society only ceased to be alarming when the brilliant Kate took them under her wing, and graciously accepted a few of their newest feathers. Well might they acquiesce, for she stood by them superbly, and her most favored partners found no way to her hand so sure as to dance systematically through that staid sisterhood. Dear,

This inexhaustible freshness of physical organization seemed to open the windows of her soul, and make for her a new heaven and earth every day. It gave also a peculiar and almost embarrassing directness to her mental processes, and suggested in them a sort of final and absolute value, as if truth had for the first time found a perfectly translucent medium. It was not so much that she said rare things, but her very silence was eloquent, and there was a great deal of it. Her girlhood had in it a certain dignity as of a virgin priestess or sibyl. Yet her hearty sympathies and her healthy energy made her at home in daily life, and in a democratic society. To Kate, for instance, she was a necessity of existence, like light or air. Kate's nature was limited; part of her graceful equipoise was narrowness. Hope was capable of far more self-abandonment to a controlling emotion, and, if she ever erred, would err more widely, for it would be because the whole power of her conscience was misdirected. "Once let her take wrong for right," said Aunt Jane, "and stop her if you can; these born saints give a great deal more trouble than children of this world, like my Kate." Yet in daily life Hope yielded to her cousin nine times out of ten; but the tenth time was the key to the situation. Hope loved Kate devotedly; but Kate believed in her as the hunted fugitive believes in the north star.

To these maidens, thus united, came Emilia home from Europe. The father of Harry and Hope had been lured into a second marriage with Emilia's mother, a charming and unscrupulous woman, born with an American body and a French soul. She having once won him to Paris, held him there life-long, and kept her step-children at a safe distance. She arranged that, even after her own death, her daughter should still remain abroad for education; nor was Emilia ordered back until she brought down some scandal by a romantic attempt to elope from boarding-school with a Swiss servant. It was by weaning her heart from this man that Philip Malbone had earned the thanks of the whole household during his hasty flight through Europe. He possessed some skill in withdrawing the female heart from an undesirable attachment, though it was apt to be done by substituting another. It was fortunate that, in this case, no fears could be entertained. Since his engagement Philip had not permitted himself so much as a flirtation; he and Hope were to be married soon; he loved and admired her heartily, and had an indifference to her want of fortune that was quite amazing, when we consider that he had a fortune of his own.

III. A DRIVE ON THE AVENUE.
OLDPORT AVENUE is a place where a great many carriages may be seen driving so slowly that they might almost be photographed without halting, and where their occupants already wear the dismal expression which befits that process. In these fine vehicles, following each other in an endless file, one sees such faces as used to be exhibited in ball-rooms during the performance of quadrilles, before round dances came in,—faces marked by the renunciation of all human joy. Sometimes a faint suspicion suggests itself on the Avenue, that these torpid countenances might be roused to life, in case some horse should run

away. But that one chance never occurs; the riders may not yet be toned down into perfect breeding, but the horses are. I do not know what could ever break the gloom of this joyless procession, were it not that youth and beauty are always in fashion, and one sometimes meets an exceptional barouche full of boys and girls, who could absolutely be no happier if they were a thousand miles away from the best society. And such a joyous company were our four youths and maidens when they went to drive that day, Emilia being left at home to rest after the fatigues of the voyage.

"What beautiful horses!" was Hope's first exclamation. "What grave people!" was her second.

> "What though in solemn silence all
> Roll round—"

quoted Philip.

"Hope is thinking," said Harry, "whether 'in reason's ear they all rejoice.'"

"How COULD you know that?" said she, opening her eyes.

"One thing always strikes me," said Kate. "The sentence of stupefaction does not seem to be enforced till after five-and-twenty. That young lady we just met looked quite lively and juvenile last year, I remember, and now she has graduated into a dowager."

"Like little Helen's kitten," said Philip. "She justly remarks that, since I saw it last, it is all spoiled into a great big cat."

"Those must be snobs," said Harry, as a carriage with unusually gorgeous liveries rolled by.

"I suppose so," said Malbone, indifferently. "In Oldport we call all new-comers snobs, you know, till they have invited us to their grand ball. Then we go to it, and afterwards speak well of them, and only abuse their wine."

"How do you know them for new-comers?" asked Hope, looking after the carriage.

"By their improperly intelligent expression," returned Phil. "They look around them as you do, my child, with the air of wide-awake curiosity which marks the American traveller. That is out of place here. The Avenue abhors everything but a vacuum."

"I never can find out," continued Hope, "how people recognize each other here. They do not look at each other, unless they know each other: and how are they to know if they know, unless they look first?"

"It seems an embarrassment," said Malbone. "But it is supposed that fashion perforates the eyelids and looks through. If you attempt it in any other way, you are lost. Newly arrived people look about them, and, the more new wealth they have, the more they gaze. The men are uneasy behind their recently educated mustaches, and the women hold their parasols with trembling hands. It takes two years to learn to drive on the Avenue. Come again next summer, and you will see in those same carriages faces of remote superciliousness, that suggest generations of gout and ancestors."

"What a pity one feels," said Harry, "for these people who still suffer from lingering modesty, and need a master to teach them to be insolent!"

"They learn it soon enough," said Kate. "Philip is right. Fashion lies in the eye. People fix their own position by the way they don't look at you."

"There is a certain indifference of manner," philosophized Malbone, "before which ingenuous youth is crushed. I may know that a man can hardly read or write, and that his father was a ragpicker till one day he picked up bank-notes for a million. No matter. If he does not take the trouble to look at me, I must look reverentially at him."

"Here is somebody who will look at Hope," cried Kate, suddenly.

A carriage passed, bearing a young lady with fair hair, and a keen, bright look, talking eagerly to a small and quiet youth beside her.

Her face brightened still more as she caught the eye of Hope, whose face lighted up in return, and who then sank back with a sort of sigh of relief, as if she had at last seen somebody she cared for. The lady waved an un-gloved hand, and drove by.

"Who is that?" asked Philip, eagerly. He was used to knowing every one.

"Hope's pet," said Kate, "and she who pets Hope, Lady Antwerp."

"Is it possible?" said Malbone. "That young creature? I fancied her ladyship in spectacles, with little side curls. Men speak of her with such dismay."

"Of course," said Kate, "she asks them sensible questions."

"That is bad," admitted Philip. "Nothing exasperates fashionable Americans like a really intelligent foreigner. They feel as Sydney Smith says the English clergy felt about Elizabeth Fry; she disturbs their repose, and gives rise to distressing comparisons,—they long to burn her alive. It is not their notion of a countess."

"I am sure it was not mine," said Hope; "I can hardly remember that she is one; I only know that I like her, she is so simple and intelligent. She might be a girl from a Normal School."

"It is because you are just that," said Kate, "that she likes you. She came here supposing that we had all been at such schools. Then she complained of us,—us girls in what we call good society, I mean,—because, as she more than hinted, we did not seem to know anything."

"Some of the mothers were angry," said Hope. "But Aunt Jane told her that it was perfectly true, and that her ladyship had not yet seen the best-educated girls in America, who were generally the daughters of old ministers and well-to-do shopkeepers in small New England towns, Aunt Jane said."

"Yes," said Kate, "she said that the best of those girls went to High Schools and Normal Schools, and learned things thoroughly, you know; but that we were only taught at boarding-schools and by governesses, and came out at eighteen, and what could we know? Then came Hope, who had been at those schools, and was the child of refined people too, and Lady Antwerp was perfectly satisfied."

"Especially," said Hope, "when Aunt Jane told her that, after all, schools did not do very much good, for if people were born stupid they only became more tiresome by schooling. She said that she had forgotten all she learned at school except the boundaries of ancient Cappadocia."

Aunt Jane's fearless sayings always passed current among her nieces; and they drove on, Hope not being lowered in Philip's estimation, nor raised in her own, by being the pet of a passing countess.

Who would not be charmed (he thought to himself) by this noble girl, who walks the earth fresh and strong as a Greek goddess, pure as Diana, stately as Juno? She belongs to the unspoiled womanhood of another age, and is wasted among these dolls and butterflies.

He looked at her. She sat erect and graceful, unable to droop into the debility of fashionable reclining,—her breezy hair lifted a little by the soft wind, her face flushed, her full brown eyes looking eagerly about, her mouth smiling happily. To be with those she loved best, and to be driving over the beautiful earth! She was so happy that no mob of fashionables could have lessened her enjoyment, or made her for a moment conscious that anybody looked at her. The brilliant equipages which they met each moment were not wholly uninteresting even to her, for her affections went forth to some of the riders and to all the horses. She was as well contented at that moment, on the glittering Avenue, as if they had all been riding home through country lanes, and in constant peril of being jolted out among the whortleberry-bushes.

Her face brightened yet more as they met a carriage containing a graceful lady dressed with that exquisiteness of taste that charms both man and woman, even if no man can analyze and no woman rival its effect. She had a perfectly high-bred look, and an eye that in an instant would calculate one's ancestors as far back as Nebuchadnezzar, and bow to them all together. She smiled good-naturedly on Hope, and kissed her hand to Kate.

"So, Hope," said Philip, "you are bent on teaching music to Mrs. Meredith's children."

"Indeed I am!" said Hope, eagerly. "O Philip, I shall enjoy it so! I do not care so very much about her, but she has dear little girls. And you know I am a born drudge. I have not been working hard enough to enjoy an entire vacation, but I shall be so very happy here if I can have some real work for an hour or two every other day."

"Hope," said Philip, gravely, "look steadily at these people whom we are meeting, and reflect. Should you like to have them say, 'There goes Mrs. Meredith's music teacher'?"

"Why not?" said Hope, with surprise. "The children are young, and it is not very presumptuous. I ought to know enough for that."

Malbone looked at Kate, who smiled with delight, and put her hand on that of Hope. Indeed, she kept it there so long that one or two passing ladies stopped their salutations in mid career, and actually looked after them in amazement at their attitude, as who should say, "What a very mixed society!"

So they drove on,—meeting four-in-hands, and tandems, and donkey-carts, and a goat-cart, and basket-wagons driven by pretty girls, with uncomfortable youths in or out of livery behind. They met, had they but known it, many who were aiming at notoriety, and some who had it; many who looked contented with their lot, and some who actually were so. They met some who put on courtesy and grace with their kid gloves, and laid away those virtues in their

15

glove-boxes afterwards; while to others the mere consciousness of kid gloves brought uneasiness, redness of the face, and a general impression of being all made of hands. They met the four white horses of an ex-harness-maker, and the superb harnesses of an ex-horse-dealer. Behind these came the gayest and most plebeian equipage of all, a party of journeymen carpenters returning from their work in a four-horse wagon. Their only fit compeers were an Italian opera-troupe, who were chatting and gesticulating on the piazza of the great hotel, and planning, amid jest and laughter, their future campaigns. Their work seemed like play, while the play around them seemed like work. Indeed, most people on the Avenue seemed to be happy in inverse ratio to their income list.

As our youths and maidens passed the hotel, a group of French naval officers strolled forth, some of whom had a good deal of inexplicable gold lace dangling in festoons from their shoulders,—"topsail halyards" the American midshipmen called them. Philip looked hard at one of these gentlemen.

"I have seen that young fellow before," said he, "or his twin brother. But who can swear to the personal identity of a Frenchman?"

IV. AUNT JANE DEFINES HER POSITION.

THE next morning had that luminous morning haze, not quite dense enough to be called a fog, which is often so lovely in Oldport. It was perfectly still; the tide swelled and swelled till it touched the edge of the green lawn behind the house, and seemed ready to submerge the slender pier; the water looked at first like glass, till closer gaze revealed long sinuous undulations, as if from unseen water-snakes beneath. A few rags of storm-cloud lay over the half-seen hills beyond the bay, and behind them came little mutterings of thunder, now here, now there, as if some wild creature were roaming up and down, dissatisfied, in the shelter of the clouds. The pale haze extended into the foreground, and half veiled the schooners that lay at anchor with their sails up. It was sultry, and there was something in the atmosphere that at once threatened and soothed. Sometimes a few drops dimpled the water and then ceased; the muttering creature in the sky moved northward and grew still. It was a day when every one would be tempted to go out rowing, but when only lovers would go. Philip and Hope went.

Kate and Harry, meanwhile, awaited their opportunity to go in and visit Aunt Jane. This was a thing that never could be done till near noon, because that dear lady was very deliberate in her morning habits, and always averred that she had never seen the sun rise except in a panorama. She hated to be hurried in dressing, too; for she was accustomed to say that she must have leisure to understand herself, and this was clearly an affair of time.

But she was never more charming than when, after dressing and breakfasting in seclusion, and then vigilantly watching her handmaiden through the necessary dustings and arrangements, she sat at last, with her affairs in order, to await events. Every day she expected something entirely new to happen, and was never disappointed. For she herself always happened, if nothing else did; she could no more repeat herself than the sunrise can; and the liveliest visitor always carried away something fresher and more remarkable than he brought.

Her book that morning had displeased her, and she was boiling with indignation against its author.

"I am reading a book so dry," she said, "it makes me cough. No wonder there was a drought last summer. It was printed then. Worcester's Geography seems in my memory as fascinating as Shakespeare, when I look back upon it from this book. How can a man write such a thing and live?"

"Perhaps he lived by writing it," said Kate.

"Perhaps it was the best he could do," added the more literal Harry.

"It certainly was not the best he could do, for he might have died,—died instead of dried. O, I should like to prick that man with something sharp, and see if sawdust did not run out of him! Kate, ask the bookseller to let me know if he ever really dies, and then life may seem fresh again."

"What is it?" asked Kate.

"Somebody's memoirs," said Aunt Jane. "Was there no man left worth writing about, that they should make a biography about this one? It is like a life of Napoleon with all the battles left out. They are conceited enough to put his age in the upper corner of each page too, as if anybody cared how old he was."

"Such pretty covers!" said Kate. "It is too bad."

"Yes," said Aunt Jane. "I mean to send them back and have new leaves put in. These are so wretched, there is not a teakettle in the land so insignificant that it would boil over them. Don't let us talk any more about it. Have Philip and Hope gone out upon the water?"

"Yes, dear," said Kate. "Did Ruth tell you?"

"When did that aimless infant ever tell anything?"

"Then how did you know it?"

"If I waited for knowledge till that sweet-tempered parrot chose to tell me," Aunt Jane went on, "I should be even more foolish than I am."

"Then how did you know?"

"Of course I heard the boat hauled down, and of course I knew that none but lovers would go out just before a thunder-storm. Then you and Harry came in, and I knew it was the others."

"Aunt Jane," said Kate, "you divine everything: what a brain you have!"

"Brain! it is nothing but a collection of shreds, like a little girl's work-basket,—a scrap of blue silk and a bit of white muslin."

"Now she is fishing for compliments," said Kate, "and she shall have one. She was very sweet and good to Philip last night."

"I know it," said Aunt Jane, with a groan. "I waked in the night and thought about it. I was awake a great deal last night. I have heard cocks crowing all my life, but I never knew what that creature could accomplish before. So I lay and thought how good and forgiving I was; it was quite distressing."

"Remorse?" said Kate.

"Yes, indeed. I hate to be a saint all the time. There ought to be vacations. Instead of suffering from a bad conscience, I suffer from a good one."

17

"It was no merit of yours, aunt," put in Harry. "Who was ever more agreeable and lovable than Malbone last night?"

"Lovable!" burst out Aunt Jane, who never could be managed or manipulated by anybody but Kate, and who often rebelled against Harry's blunt assertions. "Of course he is lovable, and that is why I dislike him. His father was so before him. That is the worst of it. I never in my life saw any harm done by a villain; I wish I could. All the mischief in this world is done by lovable people. Thank Heaven, nobody ever dared to call me lovable!"

"I should like to see any one dare call you anything else,—you dear, old, soft-hearted darling!" interposed Kate.

"But, aunt," persisted Harry, "if you only knew what the mass of young men are—"

"Don't I?" interrupted the impetuous lady. "What is there that is not known to any woman who has common sense, and eyes enough to look out of a window?"

"If you only knew," Harry went on, "how superior Phil Malbone is, in his whole tone, to any fellow of my acquaintance."

"Lord help the rest!" she answered. "Philip has a sort of refinement instead of principles, and a heart instead of a conscience,—just heart enough to keep himself happy and everybody else miserable."

"Do you mean to say," asked the obstinate Hal, "that there is no difference between refinement and coarseness?"

"Yes, there is," she said.

"Well, which is best?"

"Coarseness is safer by a great deal," said Aunt Jane, "in the hands of a man like Philip. What harm can that swearing coachman do, I should like to know, in the street yonder? To be sure it is very unpleasant, and I wonder they let people swear so, except, perhaps, in waste places outside the town; but that is his way of expressing himself, and he only frightens people, after all."

"Which Philip does not," said Hal.

"Exactly. That is the danger. He frightens nobody, not even himself, when he ought to wear a label round his neck marked 'Dangerous,' such as they have at other places where it is slippery and brittle. When he is here, I keep saying to myself, 'Too smooth, too smooth!'"

"Aunt Jane," said Harry, gravely, "I know Malbone very well, and I never knew any man whom it was more unjust to call a hypocrite."

"Did I say he was a hypocrite?" she cried. "He is worse than that; at least, more really dangerous. It is these high-strung sentimentalists who do all the mischief; who play on their own lovely emotions, forsooth, till they wear out those fine fiddlestrings, and then have nothing left but the flesh and the D. Don't tell me!"

"Do stop, auntie," interposed Kate, quite alarmed, "you are really worse than a coachman. You are growing very profane indeed."

"I have a much harder time than any coachman, Kate," retorted the injured lady. "Nobody tries to stop him, and you are always hushing me up."

"Hushing you up, darling?" said Kate. "When we only spoil you by praising and quoting everything you say."

"Only when it amuses you," said Aunt Jane. "So long as I sit and cry my eyes out over a book, you all love me, and when I talk nonsense, you are ready to encourage it; but when I begin to utter a little sense, you all want to silence me, or else run out of the room! Yesterday I read about a newspaper somewhere, called the 'Daily Evening Voice'; I wish you would allow me a daily morning voice."

"Do not interfere, Kate," said Hal. "Aunt Jane and I only wish to understand each other."

"I am sure we don't," said Aunt Jane; "I have no desire to understand you, and you never will understand me till you comprehend Philip."

"Let us agree on one thing," Harry said. "Surely, aunt, you know how he loves Hope?"

Aunt Jane approached a degree nearer the equator, and said, gently, "I fear I do."

"Fear?"

"Yes, fear. That is just what troubles me. I know precisely how he loves her. Il se laisse aimer. Philip likes to be petted, as much as any cat, and, while he will purr, Hope is happy. Very few men accept idolatry with any degree of grace, but he unfortunately does."

"Unfortunately?" remonstrated Hal, as far as ever from being satisfied. "This is really too bad. You never will do him any justice."

"Ah?" said Aunt Jane, chilling again, "I thought I did. I observe he is very much afraid of me, and there seems to be no other reason."

"The real trouble is," said Harry, after a pause, "that you doubt his constancy."

"What do you call constancy?" said she. "Kissing a woman's picture ten years after a man has broken her heart? Philip Malbone has that kind of constancy, and so had his father before him."

This was too much for Harry, who was making for the door in indignation, when little Ruth came in with Aunt Jane's luncheon, and that lady was soon absorbed in the hopeless task of keeping her handmaiden's pretty blue and white gingham sleeve out of the butter-plate.

V. A MULTIVALVE HEART.

PHILIP MALBONE had that perfectly sunny temperament which is peculiarly captivating among Americans, because it is so rare. He liked everybody and everybody liked him; he had a thousand ways of affording pleasure, and he received it in the giving. He had a personal beauty, which, strange to say, was recognized by both sexes,—for handsome men must often consent to be mildly hated by their own. He had travelled much, and had mingled in very varied society; he had a moderate fortune, no vices, no ambition, and no capacity of ennui.

He was fastidious and over-critical, it might be, in his theories, but in practice he was easily suited and never vexed.

19

He liked travelling, and he liked staying at home; he was so continually occupied as to give an apparent activity to all his life, and yet he was never too busy to be interrupted, especially if the intruder were a woman or a child. He liked to be with people of his own age, whatever their condition; he also liked old people because they were old, and children because they were young. In travelling by rail, he would woo crying babies out of their mothers' arms, and still them; it was always his back that Irishwomen thumped, to ask if they must get out at the next station; and he might be seen handing out decrepit paupers, as if they were of royal blood and bore concealed sceptres in their old umbrellas. Exquisitely nice in his personal habits, he had the practical democracy of a good-natured young prince; he had never yet seen a human being who awed him, nor one whom he had the slightest wish to awe. His courtesy, had, therefore, that comprehensiveness which we call republican, though it was really the least republican thing about him. All felt its attraction; there was really no one who disliked him, except Aunt Jane; and even she admitted that he was the only person who knew how to cut her lead-pencil.

That cheerful English premier who thought that any man ought to find happiness enough in walking London streets and looking at the lobsters in the fish-markets, was not more easily satisfied than Malbone. He liked to observe the groups of boys fishing at the wharves, or to hear the chat of their fathers about coral-reefs and penguins' eggs; or to sketch the fisher's little daughter awaiting her father at night on some deserted and crumbling wharf, his blue pea-jacket over her fair ring-leted head, and a great cat standing by with tail uplifted, her sole protector. He liked the luxurious indolence of yachting, and he liked as well to float in his wherry among the fleet of fishing schooners getting under way after a three days' storm, each vessel slipping out in turn from the closely packed crowd, and spreading its white wings for flight. He liked to watch the groups of negro boys and girls strolling by the window at evening, and strumming on the banjo,—the only vestige of tropical life that haunts our busy Northern zone. But he liked just as well to note the ways of well-dressed girls and boys at croquet parties, or to sit at the club window and hear the gossip. He was a jewel of a listener, and was not easily bored even when Philadelphians talked about families, or New Yorkers about bargains, or Bostonians about books. A man who has not one absorbing aim can get a great many miscellaneous things into each twenty-four hours; and there was not a day in which Philip did not make himself agreeable and useful to many people, receive many confidences, and give much good-humored advice about matters of which he knew nothing. His friends' children ran after him in the street, and he knew the pet theories and wines of elderly gentlemen. He said that he won their hearts by remembering every occurrence in their lives except their birthdays.

It was, perhaps, no drawback on the popularity of Philip Malbone that he had been for some ten years reproached as a systematic flirt by all women with whom he did not happen at the moment to be flirting. The reproach was unjust; he had never done anything systematically in his life; it was his temperament that flirted, not his will. He simply had that most perilous of all seductive natures, in which the seducer is himself seduced. With a personal refinement that almost amounted to purity, he was constantly drifting into loves more profoundly perilous than if they had belonged to a grosser man. Almost all women loved him, because he loved almost all; he never had to assume an ardor, for he always felt it. His heart was multivalve; he could love a dozen at once in various modes and gradations, press a dozen hands in a day, gaze into a dozen pair of eyes with unfeigned tenderness; while the last pair wept for him, he was looking into the next. In truth, he loved to explore those sweet depths; humanity is the highest thing to investigate, he said, and the proper study of mankind is woman. Woman needs to be studied while under the influence of emotion; let us therefore have the emotions. This was the reason he gave to himself; but this refined Mormonism of the heart was not based on reason, but on temperament and habit. In such matters logic is only for the by-standers.

His very generosity harmed him, as all our good qualities may harm us when linked with bad ones; he had so many excuses for doing kindnesses to his friends, it was hard to quarrel with him if he did them too tenderly. He was no more capable of unkindness than of constancy; and so strongly did he fix the allegiance of those who loved him, that the women to whom he had caused most anguish would still defend him when accused; would have crossed the continent, if needed, to nurse him in illness, and would have rained rivers of tears on his grave. To do him justice, he would have done almost as much for them,—for any of them. He could torture a devoted heart, but only through a sort of half-wilful unconsciousness; he could not bear to see tears shed in his presence, nor to let his imagination dwell very much on those which flowed in his absence. When he had once loved a woman, or even fancied that he loved her, he built for her a shrine that was never dismantled, and in which a very little faint incense would sometimes be found burning for years after; he never quite ceased to feel a languid thrill at the mention of her name; he would make even for a past love the most generous sacrifices of time, convenience, truth perhaps,—everything, in short, but the present love. To those who had given him all that an undivided heart can give he would deny nothing but an undivided heart in return. The misfortune was that this was the only thing they cared to possess.

This abundant and spontaneous feeling gave him an air of earnestness, without which he could not have charmed any woman, and, least of all, one like Hope. No woman really loves a trifler; she must at least convince herself that he who trifles with others is serious with her. Philip was never quite serious and never quite otherwise; he never deliberately got up a passion, for it was never needful; he simply found an object for his emotions, opened their valves, and then watched their flow. To love a charming woman in her presence is no test of genuine passion; let us know how much you long for her in absence. This longing had never yet seriously troubled Malbone, provided there was another charming person within an easy walk.

If it was sometimes forced upon him that all this ended in anguish to some of these various charmers, first or last, then there was always in reserve the pleasure of repentance. He was very winning and generous in his repentances, and he enjoyed them so much they were often repeated. He did not pass for a weak person, and he was not exactly weak; but he spent his life in putting away temptations with one hand and pulling them back with the other. There was for him something piquant in being thus neither innocent nor guilty, but always on some delicious middle ground. He loved dearly to skate on thin ice,—that was the trouble,—especially where he fancied the water to be just within his depth. Unluckily the sea of life deepens rather fast.

Malbone had known Hope from her childhood, as he had known her cousins, but their love dated from their meetings beside the sickbed of his mother, over whom he had watched with unstinted devotion for weary months. She had been very fond of the young girl, and her last earthly act was to place Hope's hand in Philip's. Long before this final consecration, Hope had won his heart more thoroughly, he fancied, than any woman he had ever seen. The secret of this crowning charm was, perhaps, that she was a new sensation. He had prided himself on his knowledge of her sex, and yet here was a wholly new species. He was acquainted with the women of society, and with the women who only wished to be in society. But here was one who was in the chrysalis, and had never been a grub, and had no wish to be a butterfly, and what should he make of her? He was like a student of insects who had never seen a bee. Never had he known a young girl who cared for the things which this maiden sought, or who was not dazzled by things to which Hope seemed perfectly indifferent. She was not a devotee, she was not a prude; people seemed to amuse and interest her; she liked them, she declared, as much as she liked books. But this very way of putting the thing seemed like inverting the accustomed order of affairs in the polite world, and was of itself a novelty.

Of course he had previously taken his turn for a while among Kate's admirers; but it was when she was very young, and, moreover, it was hard to get up anything like a tender and confidential relation with that frank maiden; she never would have accepted Philip Malbone for herself, and she was by no means satisfied with his betrothal to her best beloved. But that Hope loved him ardently there was no doubt, however it might be explained. Perhaps it was some law of opposites, and she needed some one of lighter nature than her own. As her resolute purpose charmed him, so she may have found a certain fascination in the airy way in which he took hold on life; he was so full of thought and intelligence; possessing infinite leisure, and yet incapable of ennui; ready to oblige every one, and doing so many kind acts at so little personal sacrifice; always easy, graceful, lovable, and kind. In her just indignation at those who called him heartless, she forgot to notice that his heart was not deep. He was interested in all her pursuits, could aid her in all her studies, suggest schemes for her benevolent desires, and could then make others work for her, and even work himself. People usually loved Philip, even while they criticised him; but Hope loved him first, and then could not criticise him at all.

Nature seems always planning to equalize characters, and to protect our friends from growing too perfect for our deserts. Love, for instance, is apt to strengthen the weak, and yet sometimes weakens the strong. Under its influence Hope sometimes appeared at disadvantage. Had the object of her love been indifferent, the result might have been otherwise, but her ample nature apparently needed to contract itself a little, to find room within Philip's heart.

Not that in his presence she became vain or petty or jealous; that would have been impossible. She only grew credulous and absorbed and blind. A kind of gentle obstinacy, too, developed itself in her nature, and all suggestion of defects in him fell off from her as from a marble image of Faith. If he said or did anything, there was no appeal; that was settled, let us pass to something else.

I almost blush to admit that Aunt Jane—of whom it could by no means be asserted that she was a saintly lady, but only a very charming one—rather rejoiced in this transformation.

"I like it better, my dear," she said, with her usual frankness, to Kate. "Hope was altogether too heavenly for my style. When she first came here, I secretly thought I never should care anything about her. She seemed nothing but a little moral tale. I thought she would not last me five minutes. But now she is growing quite human and ridiculous about that Philip, and I think I may find her very attractive indeed."

VI. "SOME LOVER'S CLEAR DAY."

"HOPE!" said Philip Malbone, as they sailed together in a little boat the next morning, "I have come back to you from months of bewildered dreaming. I have been wandering,—no matter where. I need you. You cannot tell how much I need you."

"I can estimate it," she answered, gently, "by my need of you."

"Not at all," said Philip, gazing in her trustful face. "Any one whom you loved would adore you, could he be by your side. You need nothing. It is I who need you."

"Why?" she asked, simply.

"Because," he said, "I am capable of behaving very much like a fool. Hope, I am not worthy of you; why do you love me? why do you trust me?"

"I do not know how I learned to love you," said Hope. "It is a blessing that was given to me. But I learned to trust you in your mother's sick-room."

"Ay," said Philip, sadly, "there, at least, I did my full duty."

"As few would have done it," said Hope, firmly,—"very few. Such prolonged self-sacrifice must strengthen a man for life."

"Not always," said Philip, uneasily. "Too much of that sort of thing may hurt one, I fancy, as well as too little. He may come to imagine that the balance of virtue is in his favor, and that he may grant himself a little indulgence to make up for lost time. That sort of recoil is a little dangerous, as I sometimes feel, do you know?"

"And you show it," said Hope, ardently, "by fresh sacrifices! How much trouble you have taken about Emilia! Some time, when you are willing, you shall tell me all about it. You always seemed to me a magician, but I did not think that even you could restore her to sense and wisdom so soon."

Malbone was just then very busy putting the boat about; but when he had it on the other tack, he said, "How do you like her?"

"Philip," said Hope, her eyes filling with tears, "I wonder if you have the slightest conception how my heart is fixed on that child. She has always been a sort of dream to me, and the difficulty of getting any letters from her has only added to the excitement. Now that she is here, my whole heart yearns toward her. Yet, when I look into her eyes, a sort of blank hopelessness comes over me. They seem like the eyes of some untamable creature whose language I shall never learn. Philip, you are older and wiser than I, and have shown already that you understand her. Tell me what I can do to make her love me?"

"Tell me how any one could help it?" said Malbone, looking fondly on the sweet, pleading face before him.

"I am beginning to fear that it can be helped," she said. Her thoughts were still with Emilia.

"Perhaps it can," said Phil, "if you sit so far away from people. Here we are alone on the bay. Come and sit by me, Hope."

She had been sitting amidships, but she came aft at once, and nestled by him as he sat holding the tiller. She put her face against his knee, like a tired child, and shut her eyes; her hair was lifted by the summer breeze; a scent of roses came from her; the mere contact of anything so fresh and pure was a delight. He put his arm around her, and all the first ardor of passion came back to him again; he remembered how he had longed to win this Diana, and how thoroughly she was won.

"It is you who do me good," said she. "O Philip, sail as slowly as you can." But he only sailed farther, instead of more slowly, gliding in and out among the rocky islands in the light north wind, which, for a wonder, lasted all that day,— dappling the bare hills of the Isle of Shadows with a shifting beauty. The tide was in and brimming, the fishing-boats were busy, white gulls soared and clattered round them, and heavy cormorants flapped away as they neared the rocks. Beneath the boat the soft multitudinous jellyfishes waved their fringed pendants, or glittered with tremulous gold along their pink, translucent sides. Long lines and streaks of paler blue lay smoothly along the enamelled surface, the low, amethystine hills lay couched beyond them, and little clouds stretched themselves in lazy length above the beautiful expanse. They reached the ruined fort at last, and Philip, surrendering Hope to others, was himself besieged by a joyous group.

As you stand upon the crumbling parapet of old Fort Louis, you feel yourself poised in middle air; the sea-birds soar and swoop around you, the white surf lashes the rocks far below, the white vessels come and go, the water is around you on all sides but one, and spreads its pale blue beauty up the lovely bay, or, in deeper tints, southward towards the horizon line. I know of no ruin in America which nature has so resumed; it seems a part of the living rock; you cannot imagine it away.

It is a single round, low tower, shaped like the tomb of Cacilia Metella. But its stately position makes it rank with the vast sisterhood of wave-washed strongholds; it might be King Arthur's Cornish Tyntagel; it might be "the teocallis tower" of Tuloom. As you gaze down from its height, all things that float upon the ocean seem equalized. Look at the crowded life on yonder frigate,

24

coming in full-sailed before the steady sea-breeze. To furl that heavy canvas, a hundred men cluster like bees upon the yards, yet to us upon this height it is all but a plaything for the eyes, and we turn with equal interest from that thronged floating citadel to some lonely boy in his skiff.

Yonder there sail to the ocean, beating wearily to windward, a few slow vessels. Inward come jubilant white schooners, wing-and-wing. There are fishing-smacks towing their boats behind them like a family of children; and there are slender yachts that bear only their own light burden. Once from this height I saw the whole yacht squadron round Point Judith, and glide in like a flock of land-bound sea-birds; and above them, yet more snowy and with softer curves, pressed onward the white squadrons of the sky.

Within, the tower is full of debris, now disintegrated into one solid mass, and covered with vegetation. You can lie on the blossoming clover, where the bees hum and the crickets chirp around you, and can look through the arch which frames its own fair picture. In the foreground lies the steep slope overgrown with bayberry and gay with thistle blooms; then the little winding cove with its bordering cliffs; and the rough pastures with their grazing sheep beyond. Or, ascending the parapet, you can look across the bay to the men making hay picturesquely on far-off lawns, or to the cannon on the outer works of Fort Adams, looking like vast black insects that have crawled forth to die.

Here our young people spent the day; some sketched, some played croquet, some bathed in rocky inlets where the kingfisher screamed above them, some rowed to little craggy isles for wild roses, some fished, and then were taught by the boatmen to cook their fish in novel island ways. The morning grew more and more cloudless, and then in the afternoon a fog came and went again, marching by with its white armies, soon met and annihilated by a rainbow.

The conversation that day was very gay and incoherent,—little fragments of all manner of things; science, sentiment, everything: "Like a distracted dictionary," Kate said. At last this lively maiden got Philip away from the rest, and began to cross-question him.

"Tell me," she said, "about Emilia's Swiss lover. She shuddered when she spoke of him. Was he so very bad?"

"Not at all," was the answer. "You had false impressions of him. He was a handsome, manly fellow, a little over-sentimental. He had travelled, and had been a merchant's clerk in Paris and London. Then he came back, and became a boatman on the lake, some said, for love of her."

"Did she love him?"

"Passionately, as she thought."

"Did he love her much?"

"I suppose so."

"Then why did she stop loving him?"

"She does not hate him?"

"No," said Kate, "that is what surprises me. Lovers hate, or those who have been lovers. She is only indifferent. Philip, she had wound silk upon a torn piece of his carte-de-visite, and did not know it till I showed it to her. Even then she did not care."

"Such is woman!" said Philip.

"Nonsense," said Kate. "She had seen somebody whom she loved better, and she still loves that somebody. Who was it? She had not been introduced into society. Were there any superior men among her teachers? She is just the girl to fall in love with her teacher, at least in Europe, where they are the only men one sees."

"There were some very superior men among them," said Philip. "Professor Schirmer has a European reputation; he wears blue spectacles and a maroon wig."

"Do not talk so," said Kate. "I tell you, Emilia is not changeable, like you, sir. She is passionate and constant. She would have married that man or died for him. You may think that your sage counsels restrained her, but they did not; it was that she loved some one else. Tell me honestly. Do you not know that there is somebody in Europe whom she loves to distraction?"

"I do not know it," said Philip.

"Of course you do not KNOW it," returned the questioner. "Do you not think it?"

"I have no reason to believe it."

"That has nothing to do with it," said Kate. "Things that we believe without any reason have a great deal more weight with us. Do you not believe it?"

"No," said Philip, point-blank.

"It is very strange," mused Kate. "Of course you do not know much about it. She may have misled you, but I am sure that neither you nor any one else could have cured her of a passion, especially an unreasonable one, without putting another in its place. If you did it without that, you are a magician, as Hope once called you. Philip, I am afraid of you."

"There we sympathize," said Phil. "I am sometimes afraid of myself, but I discover within half an hour what a very commonplace land harmless person I am."

Meantime Emilia found herself beside her sister, who was sketching. After watching Hope for a time in silence, she began to question her.

"Tell me what you have been doing in all these years," she said.

"O, I have been at school," said Hope. "First I went through the High School; then I stayed out of school a year, and studied Greek and German with my uncle, and music with my aunt, who plays uncommonly well. Then I persuaded them to let me go to the Normal School for two years, and learn to be a teacher."

"A teacher!" said Emilia, with surprise. "Is it necessary that you should be a teacher?"

"Very necessary," replied Hope. "I must have something to do, you know, after I leave school."

"To do?" said the other. "Cannot you go to parties?"

"Not all the time," said her sister.

"Well," said Emilia, "in the mean time you can go to drive, or make calls, or stay at home and make pretty little things to wear, as other girls do."

"I can find time for that too, little sister, when I need them. But I love children, you know, and I like to teach interesting studies. I have splendid health, and I enjoy it all. I like it as you love dancing, my child, only I like dancing too, so I have a greater variety of enjoyments."

"But shall you not sometimes find it very hard?" said Emilia.

"That is why I shall like it," was the answer.

"What a girl you are!" exclaimed the younger sister. "You know everything and can do everything."

"A very short everything," interposed Hope.

"Kate says," continued Emilia, "that you speak French as well as I do, and I dare say you dance a great deal better; and those are the only things I know."

"If we both had French partners, dear," replied the elder maiden, "they would soon find the difference in both respects. My dancing came by nature, I believe, and I learned French as a child, by talking with my old uncle, who was half a Parisian. I believe I have a good accent, but I have so little practice that I have no command of the language compared to yours. In a week or two we can both try our skill, as there is to be a ball for the officers of the French corvette yonder," and Hope pointed to the heavy spars, the dark canvas, and the high quarter-deck which made the "Jean Hoche" seem as if she had floated out of the days of Nelson.

The calm day waned, the sun drooped to his setting amid a few golden bars and pencilled lines of light. Ere they were ready for departure, the tide had ebbed, and, in getting the boats to a practicable landing-place, Malbone was delayed behind the others. As he at length brought his boat to the rock, Hope sat upon the ruined fort, far above him, and sang. Her noble contralto voice echoed among the cliffs down to the smooth water; the sun went down behind her, and still she sat stately and noble, her white dress looking more and more spirit-like against the golden sky; and still the song rang on,—

"Never a scornful word should grieve thee, I'd smile on thee, sweet, as the angels do; Sweet as thy smile on me shone ever, Douglas, Douglas, tender and true."

All sacredness and sweetness, all that was pure and brave and truthful, seemed to rest in her. And when the song ceased at his summons, and she came down to meet him,—glowing, beautiful, appealing, tender,—then all meaner spells vanished, if such had ever haunted him, and he was hers alone.

Later that evening, after the household had separated, Hope went into the empty drawing-room for a light. Philip, after a moment's hesitation, followed her, and paused in the doorway. She stood, a white-robed figure, holding the lighted candle; behind her rose the arched alcove, whose quaint cherubs looked down on her; she seemed to have stepped forth, the awakened image of a saint. Looking up, she saw his eager glance; then she colored, trembled, and put the candle down. He came to her, took her hand and kissed it, then put his hand upon her brow and gazed into her face, then kissed her lips. She quietly yielded, but her color came and went, and her lips moved as if to speak. For a moment he saw her only, thought only of her.

Then, even while he gazed into her eyes, a flood of other memories surged over him, and his own eyes grew dim. His head swam, the lips he had just kissed appeared to fade away, and something of darker, richer beauty seemed to burn through those fair features; he looked through those gentle eyes into orbs more radiant, and it was as if a countenance of eager passion obliterated that fair head, and spoke with substituted lips, "Behold your love." There was a thrill of infinite ecstasy in the work his imagination did; he gave it rein, then suddenly drew it in and looked at Hope. Her touch brought pain for an instant, as she laid her hand upon him, but he bore it. Then some influence of calmness came; there swept by him a flood of earlier, serener memories; he sat down in the window-seat beside her, and when she put her face beside his, and her soft hair touched his cheek, and he inhaled the rose-odor that always clung round her, every atom of his manhood stood up to drive away the intruding presence, and he again belonged to her alone.

When he went to his chamber that night, he drew from his pocket a little note in a girlish hand, which he lighted in the candle, and put upon the open hearth to burn. With what a cruel, tinkling rustle the pages flamed and twisted and opened, as if the fire read them, and collapsed again as if in agonizing effort to hold their secret even in death! The closely folded paper refused to burn, it went out again and again; while each time Philip Malbone examined it ere relighting, with a sort of vague curiosity, to see how much passion had already vanished out of existence, and how much yet survived. For each of these inspections he had to brush aside the calcined portion of the letter, once so warm and beautiful with love, but changed to something that seemed to him a semblance of his own heart just then,—black, trivial, and empty.

Then he took from a little folded paper a long tress of dark silken hair, and, without trusting himself to kiss it, held it firmly in the candle. It crisped and sparkled, and sent out a pungent odor, then turned and writhed between his fingers, like a living thing in pain. What part of us has earthly immortality but our hair? It dies not with death. When all else of human beauty has decayed beyond corruption into the more agonizing irrecoverableness of dust, the hair is still fresh and beautiful, defying annihilation, and restoring to the powerless heart the full association of the living image. These shrinking hairs, they feared not death, but they seemed to fear Malbone. Nothing but the hand of man could destroy what he was destroying; but his hand shrank not, and it was done.

VII. AN INTERNATIONAL EXPOSITION.

AT the celebrated Oldport ball for the French officers, the merit of each maiden was estimated by the number of foreigners with whom she could talk at once, for there were more gentlemen than ladies, and not more than half the ladies spoke French. Here Emilia was in her glory; the ice being once broken, officers were to her but like so many school-girls, and she rattled away to the admiral and the fleet captain and two or three lieutenants at once, while others hovered behind the circle of her immediate adorers, to pick up the stray shafts of what passed for wit. Other girls again drove two-in-hand, at the most, in the way of conversation; while those least gifted could only encounter one small Frenchman in some safe corner, and converse chiefly by smiles and signs.

On the whole, the evening opened gayly. Newly arrived Frenchmen are apt to be so unused to the familiar society of unmarried girls, that the most innocent share in it has for them the zest of forbidden fruit, and the most blameless intercourse seems almost a bonne fortune. Most of these officers were from the lower ranks of French society, but they all had that good-breeding which their race wears with such ease, and can unhappily put off with the same.

The admiral and the fleet captain were soon turned over to Hope, who spoke French as she did English, with quiet grace. She found them agreeable companions, while Emilia drifted among the elder midshipmen, who were dazzling in gold lace if not in intellect. Kate fell to the share of a vehement little surgeon, who danced her out of breath. Harry officiated as interpreter between the governor of the State and a lively young ensign, who yearned for the society of dignitaries. The governor was quite aware that he himself could not speak French; the Frenchman was quite unaware that he himself could not speak English; but with Harry's aid they plunged boldly into conversation. Their talk happened to fall on steam-engines, English, French, American; their comparative cost, comparative power, comparative cost per horse power,—until Harry, who was not very strong upon the steam-engine in his own tongue, and was quite helpless on that point in any other, got a good deal astray among the numerals, and implanted some rather wild statistics in the mind of each. The young Frenchman was far more definite, when requested by the governor to state in English the precise number of men engaged on board the corvette. With the accuracy of his nation, he beamingly replied, "Seeshundredtousand."

As is apt to be the case in Oldport, other European nationalities beside the French were represented, though the most marked foreign accent was of course to be found among Americans just returned. There were European diplomatists who spoke English perfectly; there were travellers who spoke no English at all; and as usual each guest sought to practise himself in the tongue he knew least. There was the usual eagerness among the fashionable vulgar to make acquaintance with anything that combined broken English and a title; and two minutes after a Russian prince had seated himself comfortably on a sofa beside Kate, he was vehemently tapped on the shoulder by Mrs. Courtenay Brash with the endearing summons: "Why! Prince, I didn't see as you was here. Do you set comfortable where you be? Come over to this window, and tell all you know!"

The prince might have felt that his summons was abrupt, but knew not that it was ungrammatical, and so was led away in triumph. He had been but a month or two in this country, and so spoke our language no more correctly than Mrs. Brash, but only with more grace. There was no great harm in Mrs. Brash; like most loquacious people, she was kind-hearted, with a tendency to corpulence and good works. She was also afflicted with a high color, and a chronic eruption of diamonds. Her husband had an eye for them, having begun life as a jeweller's apprentice, and having developed sufficient sharpness of vision in other directions to become a millionnaire, and a Congressman, and to let his wife do as she pleased.

What goes forth from the lips may vary in dialect, but wine and oysters speak the universal language. The supper-table brought our party together, and they compared notes.

"Parties are very confusing," philosophized Hope,—"especially when waiters and partners dress so much alike. Just now I saw an ill-looking man elbowing his way up to Mrs. Meredith, and I thought he was bringing her something on a plate. Instead of that, it was his hand he held out, and she put hers into it; and I was told that he was one of the leaders of society. There are very few gentlemen here whom I could positively tell from the waiters by their faces, and yet Harry says the fast set are not here."

"Talk of the angels!" said Philip. "There come the Inglesides."

Through the door of the supper-room they saw entering the drawing-room one of those pretty, fair-haired women who grow older up to twenty-five and then remain unchanged till sixty. She was dressed in the loveliest pale blue silk, very low in the neck, and she seemed to smile on all with her white teeth and her white shoulders. This was Mrs. Ingleside. With her came her daughter Blanche, a pretty blonde, whose bearing seemed at first as innocent and pastoral as her name. Her dress was of spotless white, what there was of it; and her skin was so snowy, you could hardly tell where the dress ended. Her complexion was exquisite, her eyes of the softest blue; at twenty-three she did not look more than seventeen; and yet there was such a contrast between these virginal traits, and the worn, faithless, hopeless expression, that she looked, as Philip said, like a depraved lamb. Does it show the higher nature of woman, that, while "fast young men" are content to look like well-dressed stable boys and billiard-markers, one may observe that girls of the corresponding type are apt to addict themselves to white and rosebuds, and pose themselves for falling angels?

Mrs. Ingleside was a stray widow (from New Orleans via Paris), into whose antecedents it was best not to inquire too closely. After many ups and downs, she was at present up. It was difficult to state with certainty what bad deed she had ever done, or what good deed. She simply lived by her wits, and perhaps by some want of that article in her male friends. Her house was a sort of gentlemanly clubhouse, where the presence of two women offered a shade less restraint than if there had been men alone. She was amiable and unscrupulous, went regularly to church, and needed only money to be the most respectable and fastidious of women. It was always rather a mystery who paid for her charming little dinners; indeed, several things in her demeanor were questionable, but as the questions were never answered, no harm was done, and everybody invited her because everybody else did. Had she committed some graceful forgery tomorrow, or some mild murder the next day, nobody would have been surprised, and all her intimate friends would have said it was what they had always expected.

Meantime the entertainment went on.

"I shall not have scalloped oysters in heaven," lamented Kate, as she finished with healthy appetite her first instalment.

"Are you sure you shall not?" said the sympathetic Hope, who would have eagerly followed Kate into Paradise with a supply of whatever she liked best.

"I suppose you will, darling," responded Kate, "but what will you care? It seems hard that those who are bad enough to long for them should not be good enough to earn them."

At this moment Blanche Ingleside and her train swept into the supper-room; the girls cleared a passage, their attendant youths collected chairs. Blanche tilted hers slightly against a wall, professed utter exhaustion, and demanded a fresh bottle of champagne in a voice that showed no signs of weakness. Presently a sheepish youth drew near the noisy circle.

"Here comes that Talbot van Alsted," said Blanche, bursting at last into a loud whisper. "What a goose he is, to be sure! Dear baby, it promised its mother it wouldn't drink wine for two months. Let's all drink with him. Talbot, my boy, just in time! Fill your glass. Stosst an!"

And Blanche and her attendant spirits in white muslin thronged around the weak boy, saw him charged with the three glasses that were all his head could stand, and sent him reeling home to his mother. Then they looked round for fresh worlds to conquer.

"There are the Maxwells!" said Miss Ingleside, without lowering her voice. "Who is that party in the high-necked dress? Is she the schoolmistress? Why do they have such people here? Society is getting so common, there is no bearing it. That Emily who is with her is too good for that slow set. She's the school-girl we heard of at Nice, or somewhere; she wanted to elope with somebody, and Phil Malbone stopped her, worse luck. She will be for eloping with us, before long."

Emilia colored scarlet, and gave a furtive glance at Hope, half of shame, half of triumph. Hope looked at Blanche with surprise, made a movement forward, but was restrained by the crowd, while the noisy damsel broke out in a different direction.

"How fiendishly hot it is here, though! Jones junior, put your elbow through that window! This champagne is boiling. What a tiresome time we shall have to-morrow, when the Frenchmen are gone! Ah, Count, there you are at last! Ready for the German? Come for me? Just primed and up to anything, and so I tell you!"

But as Count Posen, kissing his hand to her, squeezed his way through the crowd with Hal, to be presented to Hope, there came over Blanche's young face such a mingled look of hatred and weariness and chagrin, that even her unobserving friends saw it, and asked with tender commiseration what was up.

The dancing recommenced. There was the usual array of partners, distributed by mysterious discrepancies, like soldiers' uniforms, so that all the tall drew short, and all the short had tall. There were the timid couples, who danced with trembling knees and eyes cast over their shoulders; the feeble couples, who meandered aimlessly and got tangled in corners; the rash couples, who tore breathlessly through the rooms and brought up at last against the large white waistcoat of the violon-cello. There was the professional lady-killer, too supreme and indolent to dance, but sitting amid an admiring bevy of fair women, where he reared his head of raven curls, and pulled ceaselessly his black mustache. And there were certain young girls who, having astonished the community for a month by the lowness of their dresses, now brought to bear their only remaining art, and struck everybody dumb by appearing clothed. All these came and went and came again, and had their day or their night, and danced until the robust Hope went home exhausted and left her more fragile cousins to dance on till morning. Indeed, it was no easy thing for them to tear themselves away; Kate was always in demand; Philip knew everybody, and had that latest aroma of Paris which the soul of fashion covets; Harry had the tried endurance which befits brothers and lovers at balls; while Emilia's foreign court held out till morning, and one handsome young midshipman, in special, kept revolving back to her after each long orbit of separation, like a gold-laced comet.

The young people lingered extravagantly late at that ball, for the corvette was to sail next day, and the girls were willing to make the most of it. As they came to the outer door, the dawn was inexpressibly beautiful,—deep rose melting into saffron, beneath a tremulous morning star. With a sudden impulse, they agreed to walk home, the fresh air seemed so delicious. Philip and Emilia went first, outstripping the others.

Passing the Jewish cemetery, Kate and Harry paused a moment. The sky was almost cloudless, the air was full of a thousand scents and songs, the rose-tints in the sky were deepening, the star paling, while a few vague clouds went wandering upward, and dreamed themselves away.

"There is a grave in that cemetery," said Kate, gently, "where lovers should always be sitting. It lies behind that tall monument; I cannot see it for the blossoming boughs. There were two young cousins who loved each other from childhood, but were separated, because Jews do not allow such unions. Neither of them was ever married; and they lived to be very old, the one in New Orleans, the other at the North. In their last illnesses each dreamed of walking in the fields with the other, as in their early days; and the telegraphic despatches that told their deaths crossed each other on the way. That is his monument, and her grave was made behind it; there was no room for a stone."

Kate moved a step or two, that she might see the graves. The branches opened clear. What living lovers had met there, at this strange hour, above the dust of lovers dead? She saw with amazement, and walked on quickly that Harry might not also see.

It was Emilia who sat beside the grave, her dark hair drooping and dishevelled, her carnation cheek still brilliant after the night's excitement; and he who sat at her feet, grasping her hand in both of his, while his lips poured out passionate words to which she eagerly listened, was Philip Malbone.

Here, upon the soil of a new nation, lay a spot whose associations seemed already as old as time could make them,—the last footprint of a tribe now vanished from this island forever,—the resting-place of a race whose very funerals would soon be no more. Each April the robins built their nests around these crumbling stones, each May they reared their broods, each June the clover blossomed, each July the wild strawberries grew cool and red; all around was youth and life and ecstasy, and yet the stones bore inscriptions in an unknown language, and the very graves seemed dead.

And lovelier than all the youth of Nature, little Emilia sat there in the early light, her girlish existence gliding into that drama of passion which is older than the buried nations, older than time, than death, than all things save life and God.

VIII. TALKING IT OVER.

AUNT JANE was eager to hear about the ball, and called everybody into her breakfast-parlor the next morning. She was still hesitating about her bill of fare.

"I wish somebody would invent a new animal," she burst forth. "How those sheep bleated last night! I know it was an expression of shame for providing such tiresome food."

"You must not be so carnally minded, dear," said Kate. "You must be very good and grateful, and not care for your breakfast. Somebody says that mutton chops with wit are a great deal better than turtle without."

"A very foolish somebody," pronounced Aunt Jane. "I have had a great deal of wit in my life, and very little turtle. Dear child, do not excite me with impossible suggestions. There are dropped eggs, I might have those. They look so beautifully, if it only were not necessary to eat them. Yes, I will certainly have dropped eggs. I think Ruth could drop them; she drops everything else."

"Poor little Ruth!" said Kate. "Not yet grown up!"

"She will never grow up," said Aunt Jane, "but she thinks she is a woman; she even thinks she has a lover. O that in early life I had provided myself with a pair of twins from some asylum; then I should have had some one to wait on me."

"Perhaps they would have been married too," said Kate.

"They should never have been married," retorted Aunt Jane. "They should have signed a paper at five years old to do no such thing. Yesterday I told a lady that I was enraged that a servant should presume to have a heart, and the woman took it seriously and began to argue with me. To think of living in a town where one person could be so idiotic! Such a town ought to be extinguished from the universe."

"Auntie!" said Kate, sternly, "you must grow more charitable."

"Must I?" said Aunt Jane; "it will not be at all becoming. I have thought about it; often have I weighed it in my mind whether to be monotonously lovely; but I have always thrust it away. It must make life so tedious. It is too late for me to change,—at least, anything about me but my countenance, and that changes the wrong way. Yet I feel so young and fresh; I look in my glass every morning to see if I have not a new face, but it never comes. I am not what is called well-favored. In fact, I am not favored at all. Tell me about the party."

"What shall I tell?" said Kate.

"Tell me what people were there," said Aunt Jane, "and how they were dressed; who were the happiest and who the most miserable. I think I would rather hear about the most miserable,—at least, till I have my breakfast."

"The most miserable person I saw," said Kate, "was Mrs. Meredith. It was very amusing to hear her and Hope talk at cross-purposes. You know her daughter Helen is in Paris, and the mother seemed very sad about her. A lady was asking if something or other were true; 'Too true,' said Mrs. Meredith; 'with every opportunity she has had no real success. It was not the poor child's fault. She was properly presented; but as yet she has had no success at all.'

"Hope looked up, full of sympathy. She thought Helen must be some disappointed school-teacher, and felt an interest in her immediately. 'Will there not be another examination?' she asked. 'What an odd phrase,' said Mrs. Meredith, looking rather disdainfully at Hope. 'No, I suppose we must give it up, if that is what you mean. The only remaining chance is in the skating. I had particular attention paid to Helen's skating on that very account. How happy shall I be, if my foresight is rewarded!'

"Hope thought this meant physical education, to be sure, and fancied that handsome Helen Meredith opening a school for calisthenics in Paris! Luckily she did not say anything. Then the other lady said, solemnly, 'My dear Mrs. Meredith, it is too true. No one can tell how things will turn out in society. How often do we see girls who were not looked at in America, and yet have a great success in Paris; then other girls go out who were here very much admired, and they have no success at all.'

"Hope understood it all then, but she took it very calmly. I was so indignant, I could hardly help speaking. I wanted to say that it was outrageous. The idea of American mothers training their children for exhibition before what everybody calls the most corrupt court in Europe! Then if they can catch the eye of the Emperor or the Empress by their faces or their paces, that is called success!"

"Good Americans when they die go to Paris," said Philip, "so says the oracle. Naughty Americans try it prematurely, and go while they are alive. Then Paris casts them out, and when they come back, their French disrepute is their stock in trade."

"I think," said the cheerful Hope, "that it is not quite so bad." Hope always thought things not so bad. She went on. "I was very dull not to know what Mrs. Meredith was talking about. Helen Meredith is a warm-hearted, generous girl, and will not go far wrong, though her mother is not as wise as she is well-bred. But Kate forgets that the few hundred people one sees here or at Paris do not represent the nation, after all."

"The most influential part of it," said Emilia.

"Are you sure, dear?" said her sister. "I do not think they influence it half so much as a great many people who are too busy to go to either place. I always remember those hundred girls at the Normal School, and that they were not at all like Mrs. Meredith, nor would they care to be like her, any more than she would wish to be like them."

"They have not had the same advantages," said Emilia.

"Nor the same disadvantages," said Hope. "Some of them are not so well bred, and none of them speak French so well, for she speaks exquisitely. But in all that belongs to real training of the mind, they seem to me superior, and that is why I think they will have more influence."

"None of them are rich, though, I suppose," said Emilia, "nor of very nice families, or they would not be teachers. So they will not be so prominent in society."

"But they may yet become very prominent in society," said Hope,—"they or their pupils or their children. At any rate, it is as certain that the noblest lives will have most influence in the end, as that two and two make four."

"Is that certain?" said Philip. "Perhaps there are worlds where two and two do not make just that desirable amount."

"I trust there are," said Aunt Jane. "Perhaps I was intended to be born in one of them, and that is why my housekeeping accounts never add up."

Here hope was called away, and Emilia saucily murmured, "Sour grapes!"

"Not a bit of it!" cried Kate, indignantly. "Hope might have anything in society she wishes, if she would only give up some of her own plans, and let me choose her dresses, and her rich uncles pay for them. Count Posen told me, only yesterday, that there was not a girl in Oldport with such an air as hers."

"Not Kate herself?" said Emilia, slyly.

"I?" said Kate. "What am I? A silly chit of a thing, with about a dozen ideas in my head, nearly every one of which was planted there by Hope. I like the nonsense of the world very well as it is, and without her I should have cared for nothing else. Count Posen asked me the other day, which country produced on the whole the most womanly women, France or America. He is one of the few foreigners who expect a rational answer. So I told him that I knew very little of Frenchwomen personally, but that I had read French novels ever since I was born, and there was not a woman worthy to be compared with Hope in any of them, except Consuelo, and even she told lies."

"Do not begin upon Hope," said Aunt Jane. "It is the only subject on which Kate can be tedious. Tell me about the dresses. Were people over-dressed or under-dressed?"

"Under-dressed," said Phil. "Miss Ingleside had a half-inch strip of muslin over her shoulder."

Here Philip followed Hope out of the room, and Emilia presently followed him.

"Tell on!" said Aunt Jane. "How did Philip enjoy himself?"

"He is easily amused, you know," said Kate. "He likes to observe people, and to shoot folly as it flies."

"It does not fly," retorted the elder lady. "I wish it did. You can shoot it sitting, at least where Philip is."

"Auntie," said Kate, "tell me truly your objection to Philip. I think you did not like his parents. Had he not a good mother?"

"She was good," said Aunt Jane, reluctantly, "but it was that kind of goodness which is quite offensive."

"And did you know his father well?"

"Know him!" exclaimed Aunt Jane. "I should think I did. I have sat up all night to hate him."

"That was very wrong," said Kate, decisively. "You do not mean that. You only mean that you did not admire him very much."

"I never admired a dozen people in my life, Kate. I once made a list of them. There were six women, three men, and a Newfoundland dog."

35

"What happened?" said Kate. "The Is-raelites died after Pharaoh, or somebody, numbered them. Did anything happen to yours?"

"It was worse with mine," said Aunt Jane. "I grew tired of some and others I forgot, till at last there was nobody left but the dog, and he died."

"Was Philip's father one of them?"

"No."

"Tell me about him," said Kate, firmly.

"Ruth," said the elder lady, as her young handmaiden passed the door with her wonted demureness, "come here; no, get me a glass of water. Kate! I shall die of that girl. She does some idiotic thing, and then she looks in here with that contented, beaming look. There is an air of baseless happiness about her that drives me nearly frantic."

"Never mind about that," persisted Kate. "Tell me about Philip's father. What was the matter with him?"

"My dear," Aunt Jane at last answered,—with that fearful moderation to which she usually resorted when even her stock of superlatives was exhausted,—"he belonged to a family for whom truth possessed even less than the usual attractions."

This neat epitaph implied the erection of a final tombstone over the whole race, and Kate asked no more.

Meantime Malbone sat at the western door with Harry, and was running on with one of his tirades, half jest, half earnest, against American society.

"In America," he said, "everything which does not tend to money is thought to be wasted, as our Quaker neighbor thinks the children's croquet-ground wasted, because it is not a potato field."

"Not just!" cried Harry. "Nowhere is there more respect for those who give their lives to intellectual pursuits."

"What are intellectual pursuits?" said Philip. "Editing daily newspapers? Teaching arithmetic to children? I see no others flourishing hereabouts."

"Science and literature," answered Harry.

"Who cares for literature in America," said Philip, "after a man rises three inches above the newspaper level? Nobody reads Thoreau; only an insignificant fraction read Emerson, or even Hawthorne. The majority of people have hardly even heard their names. What inducement has a writer? Nobody has any weight in America who is not in Congress, and nobody gets into Congress without the necessity of bribing or button-holing men whom he despises."

"But you do not care for public life?" said Harry.

"No," said Malbone, "therefore this does not trouble me, but it troubles you. I am content. My digestion is good. I can always amuse myself. Why are you not satisfied?"

"Because you are not," said Harry. "You are dissatisfied with men, and so you care chiefly to amuse yourself with women and children."

"I dare say," said Malbone, carelessly. "They are usually less ungraceful and talk better grammar."

"But American life does not mean grace nor grammar. We are all living for the future. Rough work now, and the graces by and by."

"That is what we Americans always say," retorted Philip. "Everything is in the future. What guaranty have we for that future? I see none. We make no progress towards the higher arts, except in greater quantities of mediocrity. We sell larger editions of poor books. Our artists fill larger frames and travel farther for materials; but a ten-inch canvas would tell all they have to say."

"The wrong point of view," said Hal. "If you begin with high art, you begin at the wrong end. The first essential for any nation is to put the mass of the people above the reach of want. We are all usefully employed, if we contribute to that."

"So is the cook usefully employed while preparing dinner," said Philip. "Nevertheless, I do not wish to live in the kitchen."

"Yet you always admire your own country," said Harry, "so long as you are in Europe."

"No doubt," said Philip. "I do not object to the kitchen at that distance. And to tell the truth, America looks well from Europe. No culture, no art seems so noble as this far-off spectacle of a self-governing people. The enthusiasm lasts till one's return. Then there seems nothing here but to work hard and keep out of mischief."

"That is something," said Harry.

"A good deal in America," said Phil. "We talk about the immorality of older countries. Did you ever notice that no class of men are so apt to take to drinking as highly cultivated Americans? It is a very demoralizing position, when one's tastes outgrow one's surroundings. Positively, I think a man is more excusable for coveting his neighbor's wife in America than in Europe, because there is so little else to covet."

"Malbone!" said Hal, "what has got into you? Do you know what things you are saying?"

"Perfectly," was the unconcerned reply. "I am not arguing; I am only testifying. I know that in Paris, for instance, I myself have no temptations. Art and history are so delightful, I absolutely do not care for the society even of women; but here, where there is nothing to do, one must have some stimulus, and for me, who hate drinking, they are, at least, a more refined excitement."

"More dangerous," said Hal. "Infinitely more dangerous, in the morbid way in which you look at life. What have these sickly fancies to do with the career that opens to every brave man in a great nation?"

"They have everything to do with it, and there are many for whom there is no career. As the nation develops, it must produce men of high culture. Now there is no place for them except as bookkeepers or pedagogues or newspaper reporters. Meantime the incessant unintellectual activity is only a sublime bore to those who stand aside."

"Then why stand aside?" persisted the downright Harry.

"I have no place in it but a lounging-place," said Malbone. "I do not wish to chop blocks with a razor. I envy those men, born mere Americans, with no ambition in life but to 'swing a railroad' as they say at the West. Every morning I hope to wake up like them in the fear of God and the love of money."

"You may as well stop," said Harry, coloring a little. "Malbone, you used to be my ideal man in my boyhood, but"—

"I am glad we have got beyond that," interrupted the other, cheerily, "I am only an idler in the land. Meanwhile, I have my little interests,—read, write, sketch—"

"Flirt?" put in Hal, with growing displeasure.

"Not now," said Phil, patting his shoulder, with imperturbable good-nature. "Our beloved has cured me of that. He who has won the pearl dives no more."

"Do not let us speak of Hope," said Harry. "Everything that you have been asserting Hope's daily life disproves."

"That may be," answered Malbone, heartily. "But, Hal, I never flirted; I always despised it. It was always a grande passion with me, or what I took for such. I loved to be loved, I suppose; and there was always something new and fascinating to be explored in a human heart, that is, a woman's."

"Some new temple to profane?" asked Hal severely.

"Never!" said Philip. "I never profaned it. If I deceived, I shared the deception, at least for a time; and, as for sensuality, I had none in me."

"Did you have nothing worse? Rousseau ends where Tom Jones begins."

"My temperament saved me," said Philip. "A woman is not a woman to me, without personal refinement."

"Just what Rousseau said," replied Harry.

"I acted upon it," answered Malbone. "No one dislikes Blanche Ingleside and her demi monde more than I."

"You ought not," was the retort. "You help to bring other girls to her level."

"Whom?" said Malbone, startled.

"Emilia."

"Emilia?" repeated the other, coloring crimson. "I, who have warned her against Blanche's society."

"And have left her no other resource," said Harry, coloring still more. "Malbone, you have gained (unconsciously of course) too much power over that girl, and the only effect of it is, to keep her in perpetual excitement. So she seeks Blanche, as she would any other strong stimulant. Hope does not seem to have discovered this, but Kate has, and I have."

Hope came in, and Harry went out. The next day he came to Philip and apologized most warmly for his unjust and inconsiderate words. Malbone, always generous, bade him think no more about it, and Harry for that day reverted strongly to his first faith. "So noble, so high-toned," he said to Kate. Indeed, a man never appears more magnanimous than in forgiving a friend who has told him the truth.

IX. DANGEROUS WAYS.

IT was true enough what Harry had said. Philip Malbone's was that perilous Rousseau-like temperament, neither sincere enough for safety, nor false enough to alarm; the winning tenderness that thrills and softens at the mere neighborhood of a woman, and fascinates by its reality those whom no hypocrisy can deceive. It was a nature half amiable, half voluptuous, that

38

disarmed others, seeming itself unarmed. He was never wholly ennobled by passion, for it never touched him deeply enough; and, on the other hand, he was not hardened by the habitual attitude of passion, for he was never really insincere. Sometimes it seemed as if nothing stood between him and utter profligacy but a little indolence, a little kindness, and a good deal of caution.

"There seems no such thing as serious repentance in me," he had once said to Kate, two years before, when she had upbraided him with some desperate flirtation which had looked as if he would carry it as far as gentlemen did under King Charles II. "How does remorse begin?"

"Where you are beginning," said Kate.

"I do not perceive that," he answered. "My conscience seems, after all, to be only a form of good-nature. I like to be stirred by emotion, I suppose, and I like to study character. But I can always stop when it is evident that I shall cause pain to somebody. Is there any other motive?"

"In other words," said she, "you apply the match, and then turn your back on the burning house."

Philip colored. "How unjust you are! Of course, we all like to play with fire, but I always put it out before it can spread. Do you think I have no feeling?"

Kate stopped there, I suppose. Even she always stopped soon, if she undertook to interfere with Malbone. This charming Alcibiades always convinced them, after the wrestling was over, that he had not been thrown.

The only exception to this was in the case of Aunt Jane. If she had anything in common with Philip,—and there was a certain element of ingenuous unconsciousness in which they were not so far unlike,—it only placed them in the more complete antagonism. Perhaps if two beings were in absolutely no respect alike, they never could meet even for purposes of hostility; there must be some common ground from which the aversion may proceed. Moreover, in this case Aunt Jane utterly disbelieved in Malbone because she had reason to disbelieve in his father, and the better she knew the son the more she disliked the father retrospectively.

Philip was apt to be very heedless of such aversions,—indeed, he had few to heed,—but it was apparent that Aunt Jane was the only person with whom he was not quite at ease. Still, the solicitude did not trouble him very much, for he instinctively knew that it was not his particular actions which vexed her, so much as his very temperament and atmosphere,—things not to be changed. So he usually went his way; and if he sometimes felt one of her sharp retorts, could laugh it off that day and sleep it off before the next morning.

For you may be sure that Philip was very little troubled by inconvenient memories. He never had to affect forgetfulness of anything. The past slid from him so easily, he forgot even to try to forget. He liked to quote from Emerson, "What have I to do with repentance?" "What have my yesterday's errors," he would say, "to do with the life of to-day?"

"Everything," interrupted Aunt Jane, "for you will repeat them to-day, if you can."

"Not at all," persisted he, accepting as conversation what she meant as a stab. "I may, indeed, commit greater errors,"—here she grimly nodded, as if she had no doubt of it,—"but never just the same. To-day must take thought for itself."

"I wish it would," she said, gently, and then went on with her own thoughts while he was silent. Presently she broke out again in her impulsive way.

"Depend upon it," she said, "there is very little direct retribution in this world."

Phil looked up, quite pleased at her indorsing one of his favorite views. She looked, as she always did, indignant at having said anything to please him.

"Yes," said she, "it is the indirect retribution that crushes. I've seen enough of that, God knows. Kate, give me my thimble."

Malbone had that smooth elasticity of surface which made even Aunt Jane's strong fingers slip from him as they might from a fish, or from the soft, gelatinous stem of the water-target. Even in this case he only laughed good-naturedly, and went out, whistling like a mocking-bird, to call the children round him.

Toward the more wayward and impulsive Emilia the good lady was far more merciful. With all Aunt Jane's formidable keenness, she was a little apt to be disarmed by youth and beauty, and had no very stern retributions except for those past middle age. Emilia especially charmed her while she repelled. There was no getting beyond a certain point with this strange girl, any more than with Philip; but her depths tantalized, while his apparent shallows were only vexatious. Emilia was usually sweet, winning, cordial, and seemed ready to glide into one's heart as softly as she glided into the room; she liked to please, and found it very easy. Yet she left the impression that this smooth and delicate loveliness went but an inch beyond the surface, like the soft, thin foam that enamels yonder tract of ocean, belongs to it, is a part of it, yet is, after all, but a bequest of tempests, and covers only a dark abyss of crossing currents and desolate tangles of rootless kelp. Everybody was drawn to her, yet not a soul took any comfort in her. Her very voice had in it a despairing sweetness, that seemed far in advance of her actual history; it was an anticipated miserere, a perpetual dirge, where nothing had yet gone down. So Aunt Jane, who was wont to be perfectly decisive in her treatment of every human being, was fluctuating and inconsistent with Emilia. She could not help being fascinated by the motherless child, and yet scorned herself for even the doubting love she gave.

"Only think, auntie," said Kate, "how you kissed Emilia, yesterday!"

"Of course I did," she remorsefully owned. "I have kissed her a great many times too often. I never will kiss her again. There is nothing but sorrow to be found in loving her, and her heart is no larger than her feet. Today she was not even pretty! If it were not for her voice, I think I should never wish to see her again."

But when that soft, pleading voice came once more, and Emilia asked perhaps for luncheon, in tones fit for Ophelia, Aunt Jane instantly yielded. One might as well have tried to enforce indignation against the Babes in the Wood.

This perpetual mute appeal was further strengthened by a peculiar physical habit in Emilia, which first alarmed the household, but soon ceased to inspire terror. She fainted very easily, and had attacks at long intervals akin to faintness, and lasting for several hours. The physicians pronounced them cataleptic in their nature, saying that they brought no danger, and that she would certainly outgrow them. They were sometimes produced by fatigue, sometimes by excitement, but they brought no agitation with them, nor any development of abnormal powers. They simply wrapped her in a profound repose, from which no effort could rouse her, till the trance passed by. Her eyes gradually closed, her voice died away, and all movement ceased, save that her eyelids sometimes trembled without opening, and sweet evanescent expressions chased each other across her face,—the shadows of thoughts unseen. For a time she seemed to distinguish the touch of different persons by preference or pain; but soon even this sign of recognition vanished, and the household could only wait and watch, while she sank into deeper and yet deeper repose.

There was something inexpressibly sweet, appealing, and touching in this impenetrable slumber, when it was at its deepest. She looked so young, so delicate, so lovely; it was as if she had entered into a shrine, and some sacred curtain had been dropped to shield her from all the cares and perplexities of life. She lived, she breathed, and yet all the storms of life could but beat against her powerless, as the waves beat on the shore. Safe in this beautiful semblance of death,—her pulse a little accelerated, her rich color only softened, her eyelids drooping, her exquisite mouth curved into the sweetness it had lacked in waking,—she lay unconscious and supreme, the temporary monarch of the household, entranced upon her throne. A few hours having passed, she suddenly waked, and was a self-willed, passionate girl once more. When she spoke, it was with a voice wholly natural; she had no recollection of what had happened, and no curiosity to learn.

X. REMONSTRANCES.

IT had been a lovely summer day, with a tinge of autumnal coolness toward nightfall, ending in what Aunt Jane called a "quince-jelly sunset." Kate and Emilia sat upon the Blue Rocks, earnestly talking.

"Promise, Emilia!" said Kate.

Emilia said nothing.

"Remember," continued Kate, "he is Hope's betrothed. Promise, promise, promise!"

Emilia looked into Kate's face and saw it flushed with a generous eagerness, that called forth an answering look in her. She tried to speak, and the words died into silence. There was a pause, while each watched the other.

When one soul is grappling with another for life, such silence may last an instant too long; and Kate soon felt her grasp slipping. Momentarily the spell relaxed. Other thoughts swelled up, and Emilia's eyes began to wander; delicious memories stole in, of walks through blossoming paths with Malbone,—of lingering steps, half-stifled words and sentences left unfinished;—then, alas! of passionate caresses,—other blossoming paths that only showed the way to sin, but had never quite led her there, she fancied. There was so much to tell, more than could ever be explained or justified. Moment by moment, farther and farther strayed the wandering thoughts, and when the poor child looked in Kate's face again, the mist between them seemed to have grown wide and dense, as if neither eyes nor words nor hands could ever meet again. When she spoke it was to say something evasive and unimportant, and her voice was as one from the grave.

In truth, Philip had given Emilia his heart to play with at Neuchatel, that he might beguile her from an attachment they had all regretted. The device succeeded. The toy once in her hand, the passionate girl had kept it, had clung to him with all her might; he could not shake her off. Nor was this the worst, for to his dismay he found himself responding to her love with a self-abandonment of ardor for which all former loves had been but a cool preparation. He had not intended this; it seemed hardly his fault: his intentions had been good, or at least not bad. This piquant and wonderful fruit of nature, this girlish soul, he had merely touched it and it was his. Its mere fragrance was intoxicating. Good God! what should he do with it?

No clear answer coming, he had drifted on with that terrible facility for which years of self-indulged emotion had prepared him. Each step, while it was intended to be the last, only made some other last step needful.

He had begun wrong, for he had concealed his engagement, fancying that he could secure a stronger influence over this young girl without the knowledge. He had come to her simply as a friend of her Transatlantic kindred; and she, who was always rather indifferent to them, asked no questions, nor made the discovery till too late. Then, indeed, she had burst upon him with an impetuous despair that had alarmed him. He feared, not that she would do herself any violence, for she had a childish dread of death, but that she would show some desperate animosity toward Hope, whenever they should meet. After a long struggle, he had touched, not her sense of justice, for she had none, but her love for him; he had aroused her tenderness and her pride.

Without his actual assurance, she yet believed that he would release himself in some way from his betrothal, and love only her.

Malbone had fortunately great control over Emilia when near her, and could thus keep the sight of this stormy passion from the pure and unconscious Hope. But a new distress opened before him, from the time when he again touched Hope's hand. The close intercourse of the voyage had given him for the time almost a surfeit of the hot-house atmosphere of Emilia's love. The first contact of Hope's cool, smooth fingers, the soft light of her clear eyes, the breezy grace of her motions, the rose-odors that clung around her, brought back all his early passion. Apart from this voluptuousness of the heart into which he had fallen, Malbone's was a simple and unspoiled nature; he had no vices, and had always won popularity too easily to be obliged to stoop for it; so all that was noblest in him paid allegiance to Hope. From the moment they again met, his wayward heart reverted to her. He had been in a dream, he said to himself; he would conquer it and be only hers; he would go away with her into the forests and green fields she loved, or he would share in the life of usefulness for which she yearned. But then, what was he to do with this little waif from the heart's tropics,—once tampered with, in an hour of mad dalliance, and now adhering inseparably to his life? Supposing him ready to separate from her, could she be detached from him?

Kate's anxieties, when she at last hinted them to Malbone, only sent him further into revery. "How is it," he asked himself, "that when I only sought to love and be loved, I have thus entangled myself in the fate of others? How is one's heart to be governed? Is there any such governing? Mlle. Clairon complained that, so soon as she became seriously attached to any one, she was sure to meet somebody else whom she liked better. Have human hearts," he said, "or at least, has my heart, no more stability than this?"

It did not help the matter when Emilia went to stay awhile with Mrs. Meredith. The event came about in this way. Hope and Kate had been to a dinner-party, and were as usual reciting their experiences to Aunt Jane.

"Was it pleasant?" said that sympathetic lady.

"It was one of those dreadfully dark dining-rooms," said Hope, seating herself at the open window.

"Why do they make them look so like tombs?" said Kate.

"Because," said her aunt, "most Americans pass from them to the tomb, after eating such indigestible things. There is a wish for a gentle transition."

"Aunt Jane," said Hope, "Mrs. Meredith asks to have a little visit from Emilia. Do you think she had better go?"

"Mrs. Meredith?" asked Aunt Jane. "Is that woman alive yet?"

"Why, auntie!" said Kate. "We were talking about her only a week ago."

"Perhaps so," conceded Aunt Jane, reluctantly. "But it seems to me she has great length of days!"

"How very improperly you are talking, dear!" said Kate. "She is not more than forty, and you are—"

"Fifty-four," interrupted the other.

"Then she has not seen nearly so many days as you."

"But they are such long days! That is what I must have meant. One of her days is as long as three of mine. She is so tiresome!"

"She does not tire you very often," said Kate.

"She comes once a year," said Aunt Jane. "And then it is not to see me. She comes out of respect to the memory of my great-aunt, with whom Talleyrand fell in love, when he was in America, before Mrs. Meredith was born. Yes, Emilia may as well go."

So Emilia went. To provide her with companionship, Mrs. Meredith kindly had Blanche Ingleside to stay there also. Blanche stayed at different houses a good deal. To do her justice, she was very good company, when put upon her best behavior, and beyond the reach of her demure mamma. She was always in spirits, often good-natured, and kept everything in lively motion, you may be sure. She found it not unpleasant, in rich houses, to escape some of those little domestic parsimonies which the world saw not in her own; and to secure this felicity she could sometimes lay great restraints upon herself, for as much as twenty-four hours. She seemed a little out of place, certainly, amid the precise proprieties of Mrs. Meredith's establishment. But Blanche and her mother still held their place in society, and it was nothing to Mrs. Meredith who came to her doors, but only from what other doors they came.

She would have liked to see all "the best houses" connected by secret galleries or underground passages, of which she and a few others should hold the keys. A guest properly presented could then go the rounds of all unerringly, leaving his card at each, while improper acquaintances in vain howled for admission at the outer wall. For the rest, her ideal of social happiness was a series of perfectly ordered entertainments, at each of which there should be precisely the same guests, the same topics, the same supper, and the same ennui.

XI. DESCENSUS AVERNI.

MALBONE stood one morning on the pier behind the house. A two days' fog was dispersing. The southwest breeze rippled the deep blue water; sailboats, blue, red, and green, were darting about like white-winged butterflies; sloops passed and repassed, cutting the air with the white and slender points of their gaff-topsails. The liberated sunbeams spread and penetrated everywhere, and even came up to play (reflected from the water) beneath the shadowy, overhanging counters of dark vessels. Beyond, the atmosphere was still busy in rolling away its vapors, brushing the last gray fringes from the low hills, and leaving over them only the thinnest aerial veil. Farther down the bay, the pale tower of the crumbling fort was now shrouded, now revealed, then hung with floating lines of vapor as with banners.

Hope came down on the pier to Malbone, who was looking at the boats. He saw with surprise that her calm brow was a little clouded, her lips compressed, and her eyes full of tears.

"Philip," she said, abruptly, "do you love me?"

"Do you doubt it?" said he, smiling, a little uneasily.

Fixing her eyes upon him, she said, more seriously: "There is a more important question, Philip. Tell me truly, do you care about Emilia?"

He started at the words, and looked eagerly in her face for an explanation. Her expression only showed the most anxious solicitude.

For one moment the wild impulse came up in his mind to put an entire trust in this truthful woman, and tell her all. Then the habit of concealment came back to him, the dull hopelessness of a divided duty, and the impossibility of explanations. How could he justify himself to her when he did not really know himself? So he merely said, "Yes."

"She is your sister," he added, in an explanatory tone, after a pause; and despised himself for the subterfuge. It is amazing how long a man may be false in action before he ceases to shrink from being false in words.

"Philip," said the unsuspecting Hope, "I knew that you cared about her. I have seen you look at her with so much affection; and then again I have seen you look cold and almost stern. She notices it, I am sure she does, this changeableness. But this is not why I ask the question. I think you must have seen something else that I have been observing, and if you care about her, even for my sake, it is enough."

Here Philip started, and felt relieved.

"You must be her friend," continued Hope, eagerly. "She has changed her whole manner and habits very fast. Blanche Ingleside and that set seem to have wholly controlled her, and there is something reckless in all her ways. You are the only person who can help her."

"How?"

"I do not know how," said Hope, almost impatiently. "You know how. You have wonderful influence. You saved her before, and will do it again. I put her in your hands."

"What can I do for her?" asked he, with a strange mingling of terror and delight.

"Everything," said she. "If she has your society, she will not care for those people, so much her inferiors in character. Devote yourself to her for a time."

"And leave you?" said Philip, hesitatingly.

"Anything, anything," said she. "If I do not see you for a month, I can bear it. Only promise me two things. First, that you will go to her this very day. She dines with Mrs. Ingleside."

Philip agreed.

"Then," said Hope, with saddened tones, "you must not say it was I who sent you. Indeed you must not. That would spoil all. Let her think that your own impulse leads you, and then she will yield. I know Emilia enough for that."

Malbone paused, half in ecstasy, half in dismay. Were all the events of life combining to ruin or to save him? This young girl, whom he so passionately loved, was she to be thrust back into his arms, and was he to be told to clasp her and be silent? And that by Hope, and in the name of duty?

It seemed a strange position, even for him who was so eager for fresh experiences and difficult combinations. At Hope's appeal he was to risk Hope's peace forever; he was to make her sweet sisterly affection its own executioner. In obedience to her love he must revive Emilia's. The tender intercourse which he had been trying to renounce as a crime must be rebaptized as a duty. Was ever a man placed, he thought, in a position so inextricable, so disastrous? What could he offer Emilia? How could he explain to her his position? He could not even tell her that it was at Hope's command he sought her.

He who is summoned to rescue a drowning man, knowing that he himself may go down with that inevitable clutch around his neck, is placed in some such situation as Philip's. Yet Hope had appealed to him so simply, had trusted him so nobly! Suppose that, by any self-control, or wisdom, or unexpected aid of Heaven, he could serve both her and Emilia, was it not his duty? What if it should prove that he was right in loving them both, and had only erred when he cursed himself for tampering with their destinies? Perhaps, after all, the Divine Love had been guiding him, and at some appointed signal all these complications were to be cleared, and he and his various loves were somehow to be ingeniously provided for, and all be made happy ever after.

45

He really grew quite tender and devout over these meditations. Phil was not a conceited fellow, by any means, but he had been so often told by women that their love for him had been a blessing to their souls, that he quite acquiesced in being a providential agent in that particular direction. Considered as a form of self-sacrifice, it was not without its pleasures.

Malbone drove that afternoon to Mrs. Ingleside's charming abode, whither a few ladies were wont to resort, and a great many gentlemen. He timed his call between the hours of dining and driving, and made sure that Emilia had not yet emerged. Two or three equipages beside his own were in waiting at the gate, and gay voices resounded from the house. A servant received him at the door, and taking him for a tardy guest, ushered him at once into the dining-room. He was indifferent to this, for he had been too often sought as a guest by Mrs. Ingleside to stand on any ceremony beneath her roof.

That fair hostess, in all the beauty of her shoulders, rose to greet him, from a table where six or eight guests yet lingered over flowers and wine. The gentlemen were smoking, and some of the ladies were trying to look at ease with cigarettes. Malbone knew the whole company, and greeted them with his accustomed ease. He would not have been embarrassed if they had been the Forty Thieves. Some of them, indeed, were not so far removed from that fabled band, only it was their fortunes, instead of themselves, that lay in the jars of oil.

"You find us all here," said Mrs. Ingleside, sweetly. "We will wait till the gentlemen finish their cigars, before driving."

"Count me in, please," said Blanche, in her usual vein of frankness. "Unless mamma wishes me to conclude my weed on the Avenue. It would be fun, though. Fancy the dismay of the Frenchmen and the dowagers!"

"And old Lambert," said one of the other girls, delightedly.

"Yes," said Blanche. "The elderly party from the rural districts, who talks to us about the domestic virtues of the wife of his youth."

"Thinks women should cruise with a broom at their mast-heads, like Admiral somebody in England," said another damsel, who was rolling a cigarette for a midshipman.

"You see we do not follow the English style," said the smooth hostess to Philip. "Ladies retiring after dinner! After all, it is a coarse practice. You agree with me, Mr. Malbone?"

"Speak your mind," said Blanche, coolly. "Don't say yes if you'd rather not. Because we find a thing a bore, you've no call to say so."

"I always say," continued the matron, "that the presence of woman is needed as a refining influence."

Malbone looked round for the refining influences. Blanche was tilted back in her chair, with one foot on the rung of the chair before her, resuming a loud-toned discourse with Count Posen as to his projected work on American society. She was trying to extort a promise that she should appear in its pages, which, as we all remember, she did. One of her attendant nymphs sat leaning her elbows on the table, "talking horse" with a gentleman who had an undoubted professional claim to a knowledge of that commodity. Another, having finished her manufactured cigarette, was making the grinning midshipman open his lips wider and wider to receive it. Mrs. Ingleside was talking in her mincing way with a Jew broker, whose English was as imperfect as his morals, and who needed nothing to make him a millionaire but a turn of bad luck for somebody else. Half the men in the room would have felt quite ill at ease in any circle of refined women, but there was not one who did not feel perfectly unembarrassed around Mrs. Ingleside's board.

"Upon my word," thought Malbone, "I never fancied the English after-dinner practice, any more than did Napoleon. But if this goes on, it is the gentlemen who ought to withdraw. Cannot somebody lead the way to the drawing-room, and leave the ladies to finish their cigars?"

Till now he had hardly dared to look at Emilia. He saw with a thrill of love that she was the one person in the room who appeared out of place or ill at ease. She did not glance at him, but held her cigarette in silence and refused to light it. She had boasted to him once of having learned to smoke at school.

"What's the matter, Emmy?" suddenly exclaimed Blanche. "Are you under a cloud, that you don't blow one?"

"Blanche, Blanche," said her mother, in sweet reproof. "Mr. Malbone, what shall I do with this wild girl? Such a light way of talking! But I can assure you that she is really very fond of the society of intellectual, superior men. I often tell her that they are, after all, her most congenial associates. More so than the young and giddy."

"You'd better believe it," said the unabashed damsel. "Take notice that whenever I go to a dinner-party I look round for a clergyman to drink wine with."

"Incorrigible!" said the caressing mother. "Mr. Malbone would hardly imagine you had been bred in a Christian land."

"I have, though," retorted Blanche. "My esteemed parent always accustomed me to give up something during Lent,—champagne, or the New York Herald, or something."

The young men roared, and, had time and cosmetics made it possible, Mrs. Ingleside would have blushed becomingly. After all, the daughter was the better of the two. Her bluntness was refreshing beside the mother's suavity; she had a certain generosity, too, and in a case of real destitution would have lent her best ear-rings to a friend.

By this time Malbone had edged himself to Emilia's side. "Will you drive with me?" he murmured in an undertone.

She nodded slightly, abruptly, and he withdrew again.

"It seems barbarous," said he aloud, "to break up the party. But I must claim my promised drive with Miss Emilia."

Blanche looked up, for once amazed, having heard a different programme arranged. Count Posen looked up also. But he thought he must have misunderstood Emilia's acceptance of his previous offer to drive her; and as he prided himself even more on his English than on his gallantry, he said no more. It was no great matter. Young Jones's dog-cart was at the door, and always opened eagerly its arms to anybody with a title.

XII. A NEW ENGAGEMENT.

TEN days later Philip came into Aunt Jane's parlor, looking excited and gloomy, with a letter in his hand. He put it down on her table without its envelope,—a thing that always particularly annoyed her. A letter without its envelope, she was wont to say, was like a man without a face, or a key without a string,—something incomplete, preposterous. As usual, however, he strode across her prejudices, and said, "I have something to tell you. It is a fact."

"Is it?" said Aunt Jane, curtly. "That is refreshing in these times."

"A good beginning," said Kate. "Go on. You have prepared us for something incredible."

"You will think it so," said Malbone. "Emilia is engaged to Mr. John Lambert." And he went out of the room.

"Good Heavens!" said Aunt Jane, taking off her spectacles. "What a man! He is ugly enough to frighten the neighboring crows. His face looks as if it had fallen together out of chaos, and the features had come where it had pleased Fate. There is a look of industrious nothingness about him, such as busy dogs have. I know the whole family. They used to bake our bread."

"I suppose they are good and sensible," said Kate.

"Like boiled potatoes, my dear," was the response,—"wholesome but perfectly uninteresting."

"Is he of that sort?" asked Kate.

"No," said her aunt; "not uninteresting, but ungracious. But I like an ungracious man better than one like Philip, who hangs over young girls like a soft-hearted avalanche. This Lambert will govern Emilia, which is what she needs."

"She will never love him," said Kate, "which is the one thing she needs. There is nothing that could not be done with Emilia by any person with whom she was in love; and nothing can ever be done with her by anybody else. No good will ever come of this, and I hope she will never marry him."

With this unusual burst, Kate retreated to Hope. Hope took the news more patiently than any one, but with deep solicitude. A worldly marriage seemed the natural result of the Ingleside influence, but it had not occurred to anybody that it would come so soon. It had not seemed Emilia's peculiar temptation; and yet nobody could suppose that she looked at John Lambert through any glamour of the affections.

Mr. John Lambert was a millionnaire, a politician, and a widower. The late Mrs. Lambert had been a specimen of that cheerful hopelessness of temperament that one finds abundantly developed among the middle-aged women of country towns. She enjoyed her daily murders in the newspapers, and wept profusely at the funerals of strangers. On every occasion, however felicitous, she offered her condolences in a feeble voice, that seemed to have been washed a great many times and to have faded. But she was a good manager, a devoted wife, and was more cheerful at home than elsewhere, for she had there plenty of trials to exercise her eloquence, and not enough joy to make it her duty to be doleful. At last her poor, meek, fatiguing voice faded out altogether, and her husband mourned her as heartily as she would have bemoaned the demise of the most insignificant neighbor. After her death, being left childless, he had nothing to do but to make money, and he naturally made it. Having taken his primary financial education in New England, he graduated at that great business university, Chicago, and then entered on the public practice of wealth in New York.

Aunt Jane had perhaps done injustice to the personal appearance of Mr. John Lambert. His features were irregular, but not insignificant, and there was a certain air of slow command about him, which made some persons call him handsome. He was heavily built, with a large, well-shaped head, light whiskers tinged with gray, and a sort of dusty complexion. His face was full of little curved wrinkles, as if it were a slate just ruled for sums in long division, and his small blue eyes winked anxiously a dozen different ways, as if they were doing the sums. He seemed to bristle with memorandum-books, and kept drawing them from every pocket, to put something down. He was slow of speech, and his very heaviness of look added to the impression of reserved power about the man.

All his career in life had been a solid progress, and his boldest speculations seemed securer than the legitimate business of less potent financiers. Beginning business life by peddling gingerbread on a railway train, he had developed such a genius for railway management as some men show for chess or for virtue; and his accumulating property had the momentum of a planet.

He had read a good deal at odd times, and had seen a great deal of men. His private morals were unstained, he was equable and amiable, had strong good sense, and never got beyond his depth. He had travelled in Europe and brought home many statistics, some new thoughts, and a few good pictures selected by his friends. He spent his money liberally for the things needful to his position, owned a yacht, bred trotting-horses, and had founded a theological school. He submitted to these and other social observances from a vague sense of duty as an American citizen; his real interest lay in business and in politics. Yet he conducted these two vocations on principles diametrically opposite. In business he was more honest than the average; in politics he had no conception of honesty, for he could see no difference between a politician and any other merchandise. He always succeeded in business, for he thoroughly understood its principles; in politics he always failed in the end, for he recognized no principles at all. In business he was active, resolute, and seldom deceived; in politics he was equally active, but was apt to be irresolute, and was deceived every day of his life. In both cases it was not so much from love of power that he labored, as from the excitement of the game. The larger the scale the better he liked it; a large railroad operation, a large tract of real estate, a big and noisy statesman,— these investments he found irresistible.

On which of his two sets of principles he would manage a wife remained to be proved. It is the misfortune of what are called self-made men in America, that, though early accustomed to the society of men of the world, they often remain utterly unacquainted with women of the world, until those charming perils are at last sprung upon them in full force, at New York or Washington. John Lambert at forty was as absolutely ignorant of the qualities and habits of a cultivated woman as of the details of her toilet. The plain domesticity of his departed wife he had understood and prized; he remembered her household ways as he did her black alpaca dress; indeed, except for that item of apparel, she was not so unlike himself. In later years he had seen the women of society; he had heard them talk; he had heard men talk about them, wittily or wickedly, at the clubs; he had perceived that a good many of them wished to marry him, and yet, after all, he knew no more of them than of the rearing of humming-birds or orchids,— dainty, tropical things which he allowed his gardener to raise, he keeping his hands off, and only paying the bills. Whether there was in existence a class of women who were both useful and refined,—any intermediate type between the butterfly and the drudge,—was a question which he had sometimes asked himself, without having the materials to construct a reply.

With imagination thus touched and heart unfilled, this man had been bewitched from the very first moment by Emilia. He kept it to himself, and heard in silence the criticisms made at the club-windows. To those perpetual jokes about marriage, which are showered with such graceful courtesy about the path of widowers, he had no reply; or at most would only admit that he needed some elegant woman to preside over his establishment, and that he had better take her young, as having habits less fixed. But in his secret soul he treasured every tone of this girl's voice, every glance of her eye, and would have kept in a casket of gold and diamonds the little fragrant glove she once let fall. He envied the penniless and brainless boys, who, with ready gallantry, pushed by him to escort her to her carriage; and he lay awake at night to form into words the answer he ought to have made, when she threw at him some careless phrase, and gave him the opportunity to blunder.

And she, meanwhile, unconscious of his passion, went by him in her beauty, and caught him in the net she never threw. Emilia was always piquant, because she was indifferent; she had never made an effort in her life, and she had no respect for persons. She was capable of marrying for money, perhaps, but the sacrifice must all be completed in a single vow. She would not tutor nor control herself for the purpose. Hand and heart must be duly transferred, she supposed, whenever the time was up; but till then she must be free.

This with her was not art, but necessity; yet the most accomplished art could have devised nothing so effectual to hold her lover. His strong sense had always protected him from the tricks of matchmaking mammas and their guileless maids. Had Emilia made one effort to please him, once concealed a dislike, once affected a preference, the spell might have been broken. Had she been his slave, he might have become a very unyielding or a very heedless despot. Making him her slave, she kept him at the very height of bliss. This king of railways and purchaser of statesmen, this man who made or wrecked the fortunes of others by his whim, was absolutely governed by a reckless, passionate, inexperienced, ignorant girl.

And this passion was made all the stronger by being a good deal confined to his own breast. Somehow it was very hard for him to talk sentiment to Emilia;

he instinctively saw she disliked it, and indeed he liked her for not approving the stiff phrases which were all he could command. Nor could he find any relief of mind in talking with others about her. It enraged him to be clapped on the back and congratulated by his compeers; and he stopped their coarse jokes, often rudely enough. As for the young men at the club, he could not bear to hear them mention his darling's name, however courteously. He knew well enough that for them the betrothal had neither dignity nor purity; that they held it to be as much a matter of bargain and sale as their worst amours. He would far rather have talked to the theological professors whose salaries he paid, for he saw that they had a sort of grave, formal tradition of the sacredness of marriage. And he had a right to claim that to him it was sacred, at least as yet; all the ideal side of his nature was suddenly developed; he walked in a dream; he even read Tennyson.

Sometimes he talked a little to his future brother-in-law, Harry,—assuming, as lovers are wont, that brothers see sisters on their ideal side. This was quite true of Harry and Hope, but not at all true as regarded Emilia. She seemed to him simply a beautiful and ungoverned girl whom he could not respect, and whom he therefore found it very hard to idealize. Therefore he heard with a sort of sadness the outpourings of generous devotion from John Lambert.

"I don't know how it is, Henry," the merchant would gravely say, "I can't get rightly used to it, that I feel so strange. Honestly, now, I feel as if I was beginning life over again. It ain't a selfish feeling, so I know there's some good in it. I used to be selfish enough, but I ain't so to her. You may not think it, but if it would make her happy, I believe I could lie down and let her carriage roll over me. By ———, I would build her a palace to live in, and keep the lodge at the gate myself, just to see her pass by. That is, if she was to live in it alone by herself. I couldn't stand sharing her. It must be me or nobody."

Probably there was no male acquaintance of the parties, however hardened, to whom these fine flights would have seemed more utterly preposterous than to the immediate friend and prospective bridesmaid, Miss Blanche Ingleside. To that young lady, trained sedulously by a devoted mother, life was really a serious thing. It meant the full rigor of the marriage market, tempered only by dancing and new dresses. There was a stern sense of duty beneath all her robing and disrobing; she conscientiously did what was expected of her, and took her little amusements meanwhile. It was supposed that most of the purchasers in the market preferred slang and bare shoulders, and so she favored them with plenty of both. It was merely the law of supply and demand. Had John Lambert once hinted that he would accept her in decent black, she would have gone to the next ball as a Sister of Charity; but where was the need of it, when she and her mother both knew that, had she appeared as the Veiled Prophet of Khorassan, she would not have won him? So her only resource was a cheerful acquiescence in Emilia's luck, and a judicious propitiation of the accepted favorite.

"I wouldn't mind playing Virtue Rewarded myself, young woman," said Blanche, "at such a scale of prices. I would do it even to so slow an audience as old Lambert. But you see, it isn't my line. Don't forget your humble friends when you come into your property, that's all." Then the tender coterie of innocents entered on some preliminary consideration of wedding-dresses.

When Emilia came home, she dismissed the whole matter lightly as a settled thing, evaded all talk with Aunt Jane, and coolly said to Kate that she had no objection to Mr. Lambert, and might as well marry him as anybody else.

"I am not like you and Hal, you know," said she. "I have no fancy for love in a cottage. I never look well in anything that is not costly. I have not a taste that does not imply a fortune. What is the use of love? One marries for love, and is unhappy ever after. One marries for money, and perhaps gets love after all. I dare say Mr. Lambert loves me, though I do not see why he should."

"I fear he does," said Kate, almost severely.

"Fear?" said Emilia.

"Yes," said Kate. "It is an unequal bargain, where one side does all the loving."

"Don't be troubled," said Emilia. "I dare say he will not love me long. Nobody ever did!" And her eyes filled with tears which she dashed away angrily, as she ran up to her room.

It was harder yet for her to talk with Hope, but she did it, and that in a very serious mood. She had never been so open with her sister.

"Aunt Jane once told me," she said, "that my only safety was in marrying a good man. Now I am engaged to one."

"Do you love him, Emilia?" asked Hope, gravely.

"Not much," said Emilia, honestly. "But perhaps I shall, by and by."

"Emilia," cried Hope, "there is no such thing as happiness in a marriage without love."

"Mine is not without love," the girl answered. "He loves me. It frightens me to see how much he loves me. I can have the devotion of a lifetime, if I will. Perhaps it is hard to receive it in such a way, but I can have it. Do you blame me very much?"

Hope hesitated. "I cannot blame you so much, my child," she said, "as if I thought it were money for which you cared. It seems to me that there must be something beside that, and yet—"

"O Hope, how I thank you," interrupted Emilia. "It is not money. You know I do not care about money, except just to buy my clothes and things. At least, I do not care about so much as he has,—more than a million dollars, only think! Perhaps they said two million. Is it wrong for me to marry him, just because he has that?"

"Not if you love him."

"I do not exactly love him, but O Hope, I cannot tell you about it. I am not so frivolous as you think. I want to do my duty. I want to make you happy too: you have been so sweet to me."

"Did you think it would make me happy to have you married?" asked Hope, surprised, and kissing again and again the young, sad face. And the two girls went upstairs together, brought for the moment into more sisterly nearness by the very thing that had seemed likely to set them forever apart.

XIII. DREAMING DREAMS.

SO short was the period between Emilia's betrothal and her marriage, that Aunt Jane's sufferings over trousseau and visits did not last long. Mr. Lambert's society was the worst thing to bear.

"He makes such long calls!" she said, despairingly. "He should bring an almanac with him to know when the days go by."

"But Harry and Philip are here all the time," said Kate, the accustomed soother.

"Harry is quiet, and Philip keeps out of the way lately," she answered. "But I always thought lovers the most inconvenient thing about a house. They are more troublesome than the mice, and all those people who live in the wainscot; for though the lovers make less noise, yet you have to see them."

"A necessary evil, dear," said Kate, with much philosophy.

"I am not sure," said the complainant. "They might be excluded in the deed of a house, or by the terms of the lease. The next house I take, I shall say to the owner, 'Have you a good well of water on the premises? Are you troubled with rats or lovers?' That will settle it."

It was true, what Aunt Jane said about Malbone. He had changed his habits a good deal. While the girls were desperately busy about the dresses, he beguiled Harry to the club, and sat on the piazza, talking sentiment and sarcasm, regardless of hearers.

"When we are young," he would say, "we are all idealists in love. Every imaginative boy has such a passion, while his intellect is crude and his senses indifferent. It is the height of bliss. All other pleasures are not worth its pains. With older men this ecstasy of the imagination is rare; it is the senses that clutch or reason which holds."

"Is that an improvement?" asked some juvenile listener.

"No!" said Philip, strongly. "Reason is cold and sensuality hateful; a man of any feeling must feed his imagination; there must be a woman of whom he can dream."

"That is," put in some more critical auditor, "whom he can love as a woman loves a man."

"For want of the experience of such a passion," Malbone went on, unheeding, "nobody comprehends Petrarch. Philosophers and sensualists all refuse to believe that his dream of Laura went on, even when he had a mistress and a child. Why not? Every one must have something to which his dreams can cling, amid the degradations of actual life, and this tie is more real than the degradation; and if he holds to the tie, it will one day save him."

"What is the need of the degradation?" put in the clear-headed Harry.

"None, except in weakness," said Philip. "A stronger nature may escape it. Good God! do I not know how Petrarch must have felt? What sorrow life brings! Suppose a man hopelessly separated from one whom he passionately loves. Then, as he looks up at the starry sky, something says to him: 'You can bear all these agonies of privation, loss of life, loss of love,—what are they? If the tie between you is what you thought, neither life nor death, neither folly nor sin, can keep her forever from you.' Would that one could always feel so! But I am weak. Then comes impulse, it thirsts for some immediate gratification; I yield, and plunge into any happiness since I cannot obtain her. Then comes quiet again, with the stars, and I bitterly reproach myself for needing anything more than that stainless ideal. And so, I fancy, did Petrarch."

Philip was getting into a dangerous mood with his sentimentalism. No lawful passion can ever be so bewildering or ecstatic as an unlawful one. For that which is right has all the powers of the universe on its side, and can afford to wait; but the wrong, having all those vast forces against it, must hurry to its fulfilment, reserve nothing, concentrate all its ecstasies upon to-day. Malbone, greedy of emotion, was drinking to the dregs a passion that could have no to-morrow.

Sympathetic persons are apt to assume that every refined emotion must be ennobling. This is not true of men like Malbone, voluptuaries of the heart. He ordinarily got up a passion very much as Lord Russell got up an appetite,—he, of Spence's Anecdotes, who went out hunting for that sole purpose, and left the chase when the sensation came. Malbone did not leave his more spiritual chase so soon,—it made him too happy. Sometimes, indeed, when he had thus caught his emotion, it caught him in return, and for a few moments made him almost unhappy. This he liked best of all; he nursed the delicious pain, knowing that it would die out soon enough, there was no need of hurrying it to a close. At least, there had never been need for such solicitude before.

Except for his genius for keeping his own counsel, every acquaintance of Malbone's would have divined the meaning of these reveries. As it was, he was called whimsical and sentimental, but he was a man of sufficiently assured position to have whims of his own, and could even treat himself to an emotion or so, if he saw fit. Besides, he talked well to anybody on anything, and was admitted to exhibit, for a man of literary tastes, a good deal of sense. If he had engaged himself to a handsome schoolmistress, it was his fancy, and he could afford it. Moreover she was well connected, and had an air. And what more natural than that he should stand at the club-window and watch, when his young half-sister (that was to be) drove by with John Lambert? So every afternoon he saw them pass in a vehicle of lofty description, with two wretched appendages in dark blue broadcloth, who sat with their backs turned to their masters, kept their arms folded, and nearly rolled off at every corner. Hope would have dreaded the close neighborhood of those Irish ears; she would rather have ridden even in an omnibus, could she and Philip have taken all the seats. But then Hope seldom cared to drive on the Avenue at all, except as a means of reaching the ocean, whereas with most people it appears the appointed means to escape from that spectacle. And as for the footmen, there was nothing in the conversation worth their hearing or repeating; and their presence was a relief to Emilia, for who knew but Mr. Lambert himself might end in growing sentimental?

Yet she did not find him always equally tedious. Their drives had some variety. For instance, he sometimes gave her some lovely present before they set forth, and she could feel that, if his lips did not yield diamonds and rubies, his pockets did. Sometimes he conversed about money and investments, which she rather liked; this was his strong and commanding point; he explained things quite clearly, and they found, with mutual surprise, that she also had a shrewd little brain for those matters, if she would but take the trouble to think about them. Sometimes he insisted on being tender, and even this was not so bad as she expected, at least for a few minutes at a time; she rather enjoyed having her hand pressed so seriously, and his studied phrases amused her. It was only when he wished the conversation to be brilliant and intellectual, that he became intolerable; then she must entertain him, must get up little repartees, must tell him lively anecdotes, which he swallowed as a dog bolts a morsel, being at once ready for the next. He never made a comment, of course, but at the height of his enjoyment he gave a quick, short, stupid laugh, that so jarred upon her ears, she would have liked to be struck deaf rather than hear it again.

At these times she thought of Malbone, how gifted he was, how inexhaustible, how agreeable, with a faculty for happiness that would have been almost provoking had it not been contagious. Then she looked from her airy perch and smiled at him at the club-window, where he stood in the most negligent of attitudes, and with every faculty strained in observation. A moment and she was gone.

Then all was gone, and a mob of queens might have blocked the way, without his caring to discuss their genealogies, even with old General Le Breton, who had spent his best (or his worst) years abroad, and was supposed to have been confidential adviser to most of the crowned heads of Europe.

For the first time in his life Malbone found himself in the grasp of a passion too strong to be delightful. For the first time his own heart frightened him. He had sometimes feared that it was growing harder, but now he discovered that it was not hard enough.

He knew it was not merely mercenary motives that had made Emilia accept John Lambert; but what troubled him was a vague knowledge that it was not mere pique. He was used to dealing with pique in women, and had found it the most manageable of weaknesses. It was an element of spasmodic conscience than he saw here, and it troubled him.

Something told him that she had said to herself: "I will be married, and thus do my duty to Hope. Other girls marry persons whom they do not love, and it helps them to forget. Perhaps it will help me. This is a good man, they say, and I think he loves me."

"Think?" John Lambert had adored her when she had passed by him without looking at him; and now when the thought came over him that she would be his wife, he became stupid with bliss. And as latterly he had thought of little else, he remained more or less stupid all the time.

To a man like Malbone, self-indulgent rather than selfish, this poor, blind semblance of a moral purpose in Emilia was a great embarrassment. It is a terrible thing for a lover when he detects conscience amidst the armory of weapons used against him, and faces the fact that he must blunt a woman's principles to win her heart. Philip was rather accustomed to evade conscience, but he never liked to look it in the face and defy it.

Yet if the thought of Hope at this time came over him, it came as a constraint, and he disliked it as such; and the more generous and beautiful she was, the greater the constraint. He cursed himself that he had allowed himself to be swayed back to her, and so had lost Emilia forever. And thus he drifted on, not knowing what he wished for, but knowing extremely well what he feared.

XIV. THE NEMESIS OF PASSION.

MALBONE was a person of such ready, emotional nature, and such easy expression, that it was not hard for Hope to hide from herself the gradual ebbing of his love. Whenever he was fresh and full of spirits, he had enough to overflow upon her and every one. But when other thoughts and cares were weighing on him, he could not share them, nor could he at such times, out of the narrowing channel of his own life, furnish more than a few scanty drops for her.

At these times he watched with torturing fluctuations the signs of solicitude in Hope, the timid withdrawing of her fingers, the questioning of her eyes, the weary drooping of her whole expression. Often he cursed himself as a wretch for paining that pure and noble heart. Yet there were moments when a vague inexpressible delight stole in; a glimmering of shame-faced pleasure as he pondered on this visible dawning of distrust; a sudden taste of freedom in being no longer fettered by her confidence. By degrees he led himself, still half ashamed, to the dream that she might yet be somehow weaned from him, and leave his conscience free. By constantly building upon this thought, and putting aside all others, he made room upon the waste of his life for a house of cards, glittering, unsubstantial, lofty,—until there came some sudden breath that swept it away; and then he began on it again.

In one of those moments of more familiar faith which still alternated with these cold, sad intervals, she asked him with some sudden impulse, how he should feel if she loved another? She said it, as if guided by an instinct, to sound the depth of his love for her. Starting with amazement, he looked at her, and then, divining her feeling, he only replied by an expression of reproach, and by kissing her hands with an habitual tenderness that had grown easy to him,—and they were such lovely hands! But his heart told him that no spent swimmer ever transferred more eagerly to another's arms some precious burden beneath which he was consciously sinking, than he would yield her up to any one whom she would consent to love, and who could be trusted with the treasure. Until that ecstasy of release should come, he would do his duty,—yes, his duty.

When these flushed hopes grew pale, as they soon did, he could at least play with the wan fancies that took their place. Hour after hour, while she lavished upon him the sweetness of her devotion, he was half consciously shaping with his tongue some word of terrible revealing that should divide them like a spell, if spoken, and then recalling it before it left his lips. Daily and hourly he felt the last agony of a weak and passionate nature,—to dream of one woman in another's arms.

She, too, watched him with an ever-increasing instinct of danger, studied with a chilly terror the workings of his face, weighed and reweighed his words in absence, agonized herself with new and ever new suspicions; and then, when these had accumulated beyond endurance, seized them convulsively and threw them all away. Then, coming back to him with a great overwhelming ardor of affection, she poured upon him more and more in proportion as he gave her less.

Sometimes in these moments of renewed affection he half gave words to his remorse, accused himself before her of unnamed wrong, and besought her to help him return to his better self. These were the most dangerous moments of all, for such appeals made tenderness and patience appear a duty; she must put away her doubts as sins, and hold him to her; she must refuse to see his signs of faltering faith, or treat them as mere symptoms of ill health. Should not a wife cling the closer to her husband in proportion as he seemed alienated through the wanderings of disease? And was not this her position? So she said within herself, and meanwhile it was not hard to penetrate her changing thoughts, at least for so keen an observer as Aunt Jane. Hope, at length, almost ceased to speak of Malbone, and revealed her grief by this evasion, as the robin reveals her nest by flitting from it.

Yet there were times when he really tried to force himself into a revival of this calmer emotion. He studied Hope's beauty with his eyes, he pondered on all her nobleness. He wished to bring his whole heart back to her—or at least wished that he wished it. But hearts that have educated themselves into faithlessness must sooner or later share the suffering they give. Love will be avenged on them. Nothing could have now recalled this epicure in passion, except, possibly, a little withholding or semi-coquetry on Hope's part, and this was utterly impossible for her. Absolute directness was a part of her nature; she could die, but not manouvre.

It actually diminished Hope's hold on Philip, that she had at this time the whole field to herself. Emilia had gone for a few weeks to the mountains, with the household of which she was a guest. An ideal and unreasonable passion is strongest in absence, when the dream is all pure dream, and safe from the discrepancies of daily life. When the two girls were together, Emilia often showed herself so plainly Hope's inferior, that it jarred on Philip's fine perceptions. But in Emilia's absence the spell of temperament, or whatever else brought them together, resumed its sway unchecked; she became one great magnet of attraction, and all the currents of the universe appeared to flow from the direction where her eyes were shining. When she was out of sight, he needed to make no allowance for her defects, to reproach himself with no overt acts of disloyalty to Hope, to recognize no criticisms of his own intellect or conscience. He could resign himself to his reveries, and pursue them into new subtleties day by day.

There was Mrs. Meredith's house, too, where they had been so happy. And now the blinds were pitilessly closed, all but one where the Venetian slats had slipped, and stood half open as if some dainty fingers held them, and some lovely eyes looked through. He gazed so long and so often on that silent house,—by day, when the scorching sunshine searched its pores as if to purge away every haunting association, or by night, when the mantle of darkness hung tenderly above it, and seemed to collect the dear remembrances again,—that his fancy by degrees grew morbid, and its pictures unreal. "It is impossible," he one day thought to himself, "that she should have lived in that room so long, sat in that window, dreamed on that couch, reflected herself in that mirror, breathed that air, without somehow detaching invisible fibres of her being, delicate films of herself, that must gradually, she being gone, draw together into a separate individuality an image not quite bodiless, that replaces her in her absence, as the holy Theocrite was replaced by the angel. If there are ghosts of the dead, why not ghosts of the living also?" This lover's fancy so pleased him that he brought to bear upon it the whole force of his imagination, and it grew stronger day by day. To him, thenceforth, the house was haunted, and all its floating traces of herself visible or invisible,—from the ribbon that he saw entangled in the window-blind to every intangible and fancied atom she had imparted to the atmosphere,—came at last to organize themselves into one phantom shape for him and looked out, a wraith of Emilia, through those relentless blinds. As the vision grew more vivid, he saw the dim figure moving through the house, wan, restless, tender, lingering where they had lingered, haunting every nook where they had been happy once. In the windy moanings of the silent night he could put his ear at the keyhole, and could fancy that he heard the wild signals of her love and despair.

XV. ACROSS THE BAY.

THE children, as has been said, were all devoted to Malbone, and this was, in a certain degree, to his credit. But it is a mistake to call children good judges of character, except in one direction, namely, their own. They understand it, up to the level of their own stature; they know who loves them, but not who loves virtue. Many a sinner has a great affection for children, and no child will ever detect the sins of such a friend; because, toward them, the sins do not exist.

The children, therefore, all loved Philip, and yet they turned with delight, when out-door pleasures were in hand, to the strong and adroit Harry. Philip inclined to the daintier exercises, fencing, billiards, riding; but Harry's vigorous physique enjoyed hard work. He taught all the household to swim, for instance. Jenny, aged five, a sturdy, deep-chested little thing, seemed as amphibious as himself. She could already swim alone, but she liked to keep close to him, as all young animals do to their elders in the water, not seeming to need actual support, but stronger for the contact. Her favorite position, however, was on his back, where she triumphantly clung, grasping his bathing-dress with one hand, swinging herself to and fro, dipping her head beneath the water, singing and shouting, easily shifting her position when he wished to vary his, and floating by him like a little fish, when he was tired of supporting her. It was pretty to see the child in her one little crimson garment, her face flushed with delight, her fair hair glistening from the water, and the waves rippling and dancing round her buoyant form. As Harry swam farther and farther out, his head was hidden from view by her small person, and she might have passed for a red seabird rocking on the gentle waves. It was one of the regular delights of the household to see them bathe.

Kate came in to Aunt Jane's room, one August morning, to say that they were going to the water-side. How differently people may enter a room! Hope always came in as the summer breeze comes, quiet, strong, soft, fragrant, resistless. Emilia never seemed to come in at all; you looked up, and she had somehow drifted where she stood, pleading, evasive, lovely. This was especially the case where one person was awaiting her alone; with two she was more fearless, with a dozen she was buoyant, and with a hundred she forgot herself utterly and was a spirit of irresistible delight.

But Kate entered any room, whether nursery or kitchen, as if it were the private boudoir of a princess and she the favorite maid of honor. Thus it was she came that morning to Aunt Jane.

"We are going down to see the bathers, dear," said Kate. "Shall you miss me?"

"I miss you every minute," said her aunt, decisively. "But I shall do very well. I have delightful times here by myself. What a ridiculous man it was who said that it was impossible to imagine a woman's laughing at her own comic fancies. I sit and laugh at my own nonsense very often."

"It is a shame to waste it," said Kate.

"It is a blessing that any of it is disposed of while you are not here," said Aunt Jane. "You have quite enough of it."

"We never have enough," said Kate. "And we never can make you repeat any of yesterday's."

"Of course not," said Aunt Jane. "Nonsense must have the dew on it, or it is good for nothing."

"So you are really happiest alone?"

"Not so happy as when you are with me,—you or Hope. I like to have Hope with me now; she does me good. Really, I do not care for anybody else. Sometimes I think if I could always have four or five young kittens by me, in a champagne-basket, with a nurse to watch them, I should be happier. But perhaps not; they would grow up so fast!"

"Then I will leave you alone without compunction," said Kate.

"I am not alone," said Aunt Jane; "I have my man in the boat to watch through the window. What a singular being he is! I think he spends hours in that boat, and what he does I can't conceive. There it is, quietly anchored, and there is he in it. I never saw anybody but myself who could get up so much industry out of nothing. He has all his housework there, a broom and a duster, and I dare say he has a cooking-stove and a gridiron. He sits a little while, then he stoops down, then he goes to the other end. Sometimes he goes ashore in that absurd little tub, with a stick that he twirls at one end."

"That is called sculling," interrupted Kate.

"Sculling! I suppose he runs for a baked potato. Then he goes back. He is Robinson Crusoe on an island that never keeps still a single instant. It is all he has, and he never looks away, and never wants anything more. So I have him to watch. Think of living so near a beaver or a water-rat with clothes on! Good-by. Leave the door ajar, it is so warm."

And Kate went down to the landing. It was near the "baptismal shore," where every Sunday the young people used to watch the immersions; they liked to see the crowd of spectators, the eager friends, the dripping convert, the serene young minister, the old men and girls who burst forth in song as the new disciple rose from the waves. It was the weekly festival in that region, and the sunshine and the ripples made it gladdening, not gloomy. Every other day in the week the children of the fishermen waded waist-deep in the water, and played at baptism.

Near this shore stood the family bathing-house; and the girls came down to sit in its shadow and watch the swimming. It was late in August, and on the first of September Emilia was to be married.

Nothing looked cool, that day, but the bay and those who were going into it. Out came Hope from the bathing-house, in a new bathing-dress of dark blue, which was evidently what the others had come forth to behold.

"Hope, what an imposter you are!" cried Kate instantly. "You declined all my proffers of aid in cutting that dress, and now see how it fits you! You never looked so beautifully in your life. There is not such another bathing-dress in Oldport, nor such a figure to wear it."

And she put both her arms round that supple, stately waist, that might have belonged to a Greek goddess, or to some queen in the Nibelungen Lied.

The party watched the swimmers as they struck out over the clear expanse. It was high noon; the fishing-boats were all off, but a few pleasure-boats swung different ways at their moorings, in the perfect calm. The white light-house stood reflected opposite, at the end of its long pier; a few vessels lay at anchor, with their sails up to dry, but with that deserted look which coasters in port are wont to wear. A few fishes dimpled the still surface, and as the three swam out farther and farther, their merry voices still sounded close at hand. Suddenly they all clapped their hands and called; then pointed forward to the light-house, across the narrow harbor.

"They are going to swim across," said Kate. "What creatures they are! Hope and little Jenny have always begged for it, and now Harry thinks it is so still a day they can safely venture. It is more than half a mile. See! he has called that boy in a boat, and he will keep near them. They have swum farther than that along the shore."

So the others went away with no fears.

Hope said afterwards that she never swam with such delight as on that day. The water seemed to be peculiarly thin and clear, she said, as well as tranquil, and to retain its usual buoyancy without its density. It gave a delicious sense of freedom; she seemed to swim in air, and felt singularly secure. For the first time she felt what she had always wished to experience,—that swimming was as natural as walking, and might be indefinitely prolonged. Her strength seemed limitless, she struck out more and more strongly; she splashed and played with little Jenny, when the child began to grow weary of the long motion. A fisherman's boy in a boat rowed slowly along by their side.

Nine tenths of the distance had been accomplished, when the little girl grew quite impatient, and Hope bade Harry swim on before her, and land his charge. Light and buoyant as the child was, her tightened clasp had begun to tell on him.

"It tires you, Hal, to bear that weight so long, and you know I have nothing to carry. You must see that I am not in the least tired, only a little dazzled by the sun. Here, Charley, give me your hat, and then row on with Mr. Harry." She put on the boy's torn straw hat, and they yielded to her wish. People almost always yielded to Hope's wishes when she expressed them,—it was so very seldom.

Somehow the remaining distance seemed very great, as Hope saw them glide away, leaving her in the water alone, her feet unsupported by any firm element, the bright and pitiless sky arching far above her, and her head burning with more heat than she had liked to own. She was conscious of her full strength, and swam more vigorously than ever; but her head was hot and her ears rang, and she felt chilly vibrations passing up and down her sides, that were like, she fancied, the innumerable fringing oars of the little jelly-fishes she had so often watched. Her body felt almost unnaturally strong, and she took powerful strokes; but it seemed as if her heart went out into them and left a vacant cavity within. More and more her life seemed boiling up into her head; queer fancies came to her, as, for instance, that she was an inverted thermometer with the mercury all ascending into a bulb at the top. She shook her head and the fancy cleared away, and then others came.

She began to grow seriously anxious, but the distance was diminishing; Harry was almost at the steps with the child, and the boy had rowed his skiff round the breakwater out of sight; a young fisherman leaned over the railing with his back to her, watching the lobster-catchers on the other side. She was almost in; it was only a slight dizziness, yet she could not see the light-house. Concentrating all her efforts, she shut her eyes and swam on, her arms still unaccountably vigorous, though the rest of her body seemed losing itself in languor. The sound in her ear had grown to a roar, as of many mill-wheels. It seemed a long distance that she thus swam with her eyes closed. Then she half opened her eyes, and the breakwater seemed all in motion, with tier above tier of eager faces looking down on her. In an instant there was a sharp splash close beside her, and she felt herself grasped and drawn downwards, with a whirl of something just above her, and then all consciousness went out as suddenly as when ether brings at last to a patient, after the roaring and the tumult in his brain, its blessed foretaste of the deliciousness of death.

When Hope came again to consciousness, she found herself approaching her own pier in a sail-boat, with several very wet gentlemen around her, and little Jenny nestled close to her, crying as profusely as if her pretty scarlet bathing-dress were being wrung out through her eyes. Hope asked no questions, and hardly felt the impulse to inquire what had happened. The truth was, that in the temporary dizziness produced by her prolonged swim, she had found herself in the track of a steamboat that was passing the pier, unobserved by her brother. A young man, leaping from the dock, had caught her in his arms, and had dived with her below the paddle-wheels, just as they came upon her. It was a daring act, but nothing else could have saved her. When they came to the surface, they had been picked up by Aunt Jane's Robinson Crusoe, who had at last unmoored his pilot-boat and was rounding the light-house for the outer harbor.

She and the child were soon landed, and given over to the ladies. Due attention was paid to her young rescuer, whose dripping garments seemed for the moment as glorious as a blood-stained flag. He seemed a simple, frank young fellow of

61

French or German origin, but speaking English remarkably well; he was not high-bred, by any means, but had apparently the culture of an average German of the middle class. Harry fancied that he had seen him before, and at last traced back the impression of his features to the ball for the French officers. It turned out, on inquiry, that he had a brother in the service, and on board the corvette; but he himself was a commercial agent, now in America with a view to business, though he had made several voyages as mate of a vessel, and would not object to some such berth as that. He promised to return and receive the thanks of the family, read with interest the name on Harry's card, seemed about to ask a question, but forbore, and took his leave amid the general confusion, without even giving his address. When sought next day, he was not to be found, and to the children he at once became as much a creature of romance as the sea-serpent or the Flying Dutchman.

Even Hope's strong constitution felt the shock of this adventure. She was confined to her room for a week or two, but begged that there might be no postponement of the wedding, which, therefore, took place without her. Her illness gave excuse for a privacy that was welcome to all but the bridesmaids, and suited Malbone best of all.

XVI. ON THE STAIRS.

AUGUST drew toward its close, and guests departed from the neighborhood.

"What a short little thing summer is," meditated Aunt Jane, "and butterflies are caterpillars most of the time after all. How quiet it seems. The wrens whisper in their box above the window, and there has not been a blast from the peacock for a week. He seems ashamed of the summer shortness of his tail. He keeps glancing at it over his shoulder to see if it is not looking better than yesterday, while the staring eyes of the old tail are in the bushes all about."

"Poor, dear little thing!" said coaxing Katie. "Is she tired of autumn, before it is begun?"

"I am never tired of anything," said Aunt Jane, "except my maid Ruth, and I should not be tired of her, if it had pleased Heaven to endow her with sufficient strength of mind to sew on a button. Life is very rich to me. There is always something new in every season; though to be sure I cannot think what novelty there is just now, except a choice variety of spiders. There is a theory that spiders kill flies. But I never miss a fly, and there does not seem to be any natural scourge divinely appointed to kill spiders, except Ruth. Even she does it so feebly, that I see them come back and hang on their webs and make faces at her. I suppose they are faces; I do not understand their anatomy, but it must be a very unpleasant one."

"You are not quite satisfied with life, today, dear," said Kate; "I fear your book did not end to your satisfaction."

"It did end, though," said the lady, "and that is something. What is there in life so difficult as to stop a book? If I wrote one, it would be as long as ten 'Sir

Charles Grandisons,' and then I never should end it, because I should die. And there would be nobody left to read it, because each reader would have been dead long before."

"But the book amused you!" interrupted Kate. "I know it did."

"It was so absurd that I laughed till I cried; and it makes no difference whether you cry laughing or cry crying; it is equally bad when your glasses come off. Never mind. Whom did you see on the Avenue?"

"O, we saw Philip on horseback. He rides so beautifully; he seems one with his horse."

"I am glad of it," interposed his aunt. "The riders are generally so inferior to them."

"We saw Mr. and Mrs. Lambert, too. Emilia stopped and asked after you, and sent you her love, auntie."

"Love!" cried Aunt Jane. "She always does that. She has sent me love enough to rear a whole family on,—more than I ever felt for anybody in all my days. But she does not really love any one."

"I hope she will love her husband," said Kate, rather seriously.

"Mark my words, Kate!" said her aunt. "Nothing but unhappiness will ever come of that marriage. How can two people be happy who have absolutely nothing in common?"

"But no two people have just the same tastes," said Kate, "except Harry and myself. It is not expected. It would be absurd for two people to be divorced, because the one preferred white bread and the other brown."

"They would be divorced very soon," said Aunt Jane, "for the one who ate brown bread would not live long."

"But it is possible that he might live, auntie, in spite of your prediction. And perhaps people may be happy, even if you and I do not see how."

"Nobody ever thinks I see anything," said Aunt Jane, in some dejection. "You think I am nothing in the world but a sort of old oyster, making amusement for people, and having no more to do with real life than oysters have."

"No, dearest!" cried Kate. "You have a great deal to do with all our lives. You are a dear old insidious sapper-and-miner, looking at first very inoffensive, and then working your way into our affections, and spoiling us with coaxing. How you behave about children, for instance!"

"How?" said the other meekly. "As well as I can."

"But you pretend that you dislike them."

"But I do dislike them. How can anybody help it? Hear them swearing at this moment, boys of five, paddling in the water there! Talk about the murder of the innocents! There are so few innocents to be murdered! If I only had a gun and could shoot!"

"You may not like those particular boys," said Kate, "but you like good, well-behaved children, very much."

"It takes so many to take care of them! People drive by here, with carriages so large that two of the largest horses can hardly draw them, and all full of those little beings. They have a sort of roof, too, and seem to expect to be out in all weathers."

"If you had a family of children, perhaps you would find such a travelling caravan very convenient," said Kate.

"If I had such a family," said her aunt, "I would have a separate governess and guardian for each, very moral persons. They should come when each child was two, and stay till it was twenty. The children should all live apart, in order not to quarrel, and should meet once or twice a day and bow to each other. I think that each should learn a different language, so as not to converse, and then, perhaps, they would not get each other into mischief."

"I am sure, auntie," said Kate, "you have missed our small nephews and nieces ever since their visit ended. How still the house has been!"

"I do not know," was the answer. "I hear a great many noises about the house. Somebody comes in late at night. Perhaps it is Philip; but he comes very softly in, wipes his feet very gently, like a clean thief, and goes up stairs."

"O auntie!" said Kate, "you know you have got over all such fancies."

"They are not fancies," said Aunt Jane. "Things do happen in houses! Did I not look under the bed for a thief during fifteen years, and find one at last? Why should I not be allowed to hear something now?"

"But, dear Aunt Jane," said Kate, "you never told me this before."

"No," said she. "I was beginning to tell you the other day, but Ruth was just bringing in my handkerchiefs, and she had used so much bluing, they looked as if they had been washed in heaven, so that it was too outrageous, and I forgot everything else."

"But do you really hear anything?"

"Yes," said her aunt. "Ruth declares she hears noises in those closets that I had nailed up, you know; but that is nothing; of course she does. Rats. What I hear at night is the creaking of stairs, when I know that nobody ought to be stirring. If you observe, you will hear it too. At least, I should think you would, only that somehow everything always seems to stop, when it is necessary to prove that I am foolish."

The girls had no especial engagement that evening, and so got into a great excitement on the stairway over Aunt Jane's solicitudes. They convinced themselves that they heard all sorts of things,—footfalls on successive steps, the creak of a plank, the brushing of an arm against a wall, the jar of some suspended object that was stirred in passing. Once they heard something fall on the floor, and roll from step to step; and yet they themselves stood on the stairway, and nothing passed. Then for some time there was silence, but they would have persisted in their observations, had not Philip come in from Mrs. Meredith's in the midst of it, so that the whole thing turned into a frolic, and they sat on the stairs and told ghost stories half the night.

XVII. DISCOVERY.

THE next evening Kate and Philip went to a ball. As Hope was passing through the hall late in the evening, she heard a sudden, sharp cry somewhere in the upper regions, that sounded, she thought, like a woman's voice. She stopped to hear, but there was silence. It seemed to come from the direction of Malbone's room, which was in the third story. Again came the cry, more gently, ending in a sort of sobbing monologue. Gliding rapidly up stairs in the dark, she paused at Philip's deserted room, but the door was locked, and there was profound stillness. She then descended, and pausing at the great landing, heard other steps descending also. Retreating to the end of the hall, she hastily lighted a candle, when the steps ceased. With her accustomed nerve, wishing to explore the thing thoroughly, she put out the light and kept still. As she expected, the footsteps presently recommenced, descending stealthily, but drawing no nearer, and seeming rather like sounds from an adjoining house, heard through a party-wall. This was impossible, as the house stood alone. Flushed with excitement, she relighted the hall candles, and, taking one of them, searched the whole entry and stairway, going down even to the large, old-fashioned cellar.

Looking about her in this unfamiliar region, her eye fell on a door that seemed to open into the wall; she had noticed a similar door on the story above,—one of the closet doors that had been nailed up by Aunt Jane's order. As she looked, however, a chill breath blew in from another direction, extinguishing her lamp. This air came from the outer door of the cellar, and she had just time to withdraw into a corner before a man's steps approached, passing close by her.

Even Hope's strong nerves had begun to yield, and a cold shudder went through her. Not daring to move, she pressed herself against the wall, and her heart seemed to stop as the unseen stranger passed. Instead of his ascending where she had come down, as she had expected, she heard him grope his way toward the door she had seen in the wall.

There he seemed to find a stairway, and when his steps were thus turned from her, she was seized by a sudden impulse and followed him, groping her way as she could. She remembered that the girls had talked of secret stairways in that house, though she had no conception whither they could lead, unless to some of the shut-up closets.

She steadily followed, treading cautiously upon each creaking step. The stairway was very narrow, and formed a regular spiral as in a turret. The darkness and the curving motion confused her brain, and it was impossible to tell how high in the house she was, except when once she put her hand upon what was evidently a door, and moreover saw through its cracks the lamp she had left burning in the upper hall. This glimpse of reality reassured her. She had begun to discover where she was. The doors which Aunt Jane had closed gave access, not to mere closets, but to a spiral stairway, which evidently went from top to bottom of the house, and was known to some one else beside herself.

Relieved of that slight shudder at the supernatural which sometimes affects the healthiest nerves, Hope paused to consider. To alarm the neighborhood was her first thought. A slight murmuring from above dispelled it; she must first reconnoitre a few steps farther. As she ascended a little way, a gleam shone upon her, and down the damp stairway came a fragrant odor, as from some perfumed chamber. Then a door was shut and reopened. Eager beyond expression, she followed on. Another step, and she stood at the door of Malbone's apartment.

65

The room was brilliant with light; the doors and windows were heavily draped. Fruit and flowers and wine were on the table. On the sofa lay Emilia in a gay ball-dress, sunk in one of her motionless trances, while Malbone, pale with terror, was deluging her brows with the water he had just brought from the well below.

Hope stopped a moment and leaned against the door, as her eyes met Malbone's. Then she made her way to a chair, and leaning on the back of it, which she fingered convulsively, looked with bewildered eyes and compressed lips from the one to the other. Malbone tried to speak, but failed; tried again, and brought forth only a whisper that broke into clearer speech as the words went on. "No use to explain," he said. "Lambert is in New York. Mrs. Meredith is expecting her—to-night after the ball. What can we do?"

Hope covered her face as he spoke; she could bear anything better than to have him say "we," as if no gulf had opened between them. She sank slowly on her knees behind her chair, keeping it as a sort of screen between herself and these two people,—the counterfeits, they seemed, of her lover and her sister. If the roof in falling to crush them had crushed her also, she could scarcely have seemed more rigid or more powerless. It passed, and the next moment she was on her feet again, capable of action.

"She must be taken," she said very clearly, but in a lower tone than usual, "to my chamber." Then pointing to the candles, she said, more huskily, "We must not be seen. Put them out." Every syllable seemed to exhaust her. But as Philip obeyed her words, he saw her move suddenly and stand by Emilia's side.

She put out both arms as if to lift the young girl, and carry her away.

"You cannot," said Philip, putting her gently aside, while she shrank from his touch. Then he took Emilia in his arms and bore her to the door, Hope preceding.

Motioning him to pause a moment, she turned the lock softly, and looked out into the dark entry. All was still. She went out, and he followed with his motionless burden. They walked stealthily, like guilty things, yet every slight motion seemed to ring in their ears. It was chilly, and Hope shivered. Through the great open window on the stairway a white fog peered in at them, and the distant fog-whistle came faintly through; it seemed as if the very atmosphere were condensing about them, to isolate the house in which such deeds were done. The clock struck twelve, and it seemed as if it struck a thousand.

When they reached Hope's door, she turned and put out her arms for Emilia, as for a child. Every expression had now gone from Hope's face but a sort of stony calmness, which put her infinitely farther from Malbone than had the momentary struggle. As he gave the girlish form into arms that shook and trembled beneath its weight, he caught a glimpse in the pier-glass of their two white faces, and then, looking down, saw the rose-tints yet lingering on Emilia's cheek. She, the source of all this woe, looked the only representative of innocence between two guilty things.

How white and pure and maidenly looked Hope's little room,—such a home of peace, he thought, till its door suddenly opened to admit all this passion and despair! There was a great sheaf of cardinal flowers on the table, and their petals were drooping, as if reluctant to look on him. Scheffer's Christus Consolator was upon the walls, and the benign figure seemed to spread wider its arms of mercy, to take in a few sad hearts more.

Hope bore Emilia into the light and purity and warmth, while Malbone was shut out into the darkness and the chill. The only two things to which he clung on earth, the two women between whom his unsteady heart had vibrated, and both whose lives had been tortured by its vacillation, went away from his sight together, the one victim bearing the other victim in her arms. Never any more while he lived would either of them be his again; and had Dante known it for his last glimpse of things immortal when the two lovers floated away from him in their sad embrace, he would have had no such sense of utter banishment as had Malbone then.

XVIII. HOPE'S VIGIL.

HAD Emilia chosen out of life's whole armory of weapons the means of disarming Hope, she could have found nothing so effectual as nature had supplied in her unconsciousness. Helplessness conquers. There was a quality in Emilia which would have always produced something very like antagonism in Hope, had she not been her sister. Had the ungoverned girl now been able to utter one word of reproach, had her eyes flashed one look of defiance, had her hand made one triumphant or angry gesture, perhaps all Hope's outraged womanhood would have coldly nerved itself against her. But it was another thing to see those soft eyes closed, those delicate hands powerless, those pleading lips sealed; to see her extended in graceful helplessness, while all the concentrated drama of emotion revolved around her unheeded, as around Cordelia dead. In what realms was that child's mind seeking comfort; through what thin air of dreams did that restless heart beat its pinions; in what other sphere did that untamed nature wander, while shame and sorrow waited for its awakening in this?

Hope knelt upon the floor, still too much strained and bewildered for tears or even prayer, a little way from Emilia. Once having laid down the unconscious form, it seemed for a moment as if she could no more touch it than she could lay her hand amid flames. A gap of miles, of centuries, of solar systems, seemed to separate these two young girls, alone within the same chamber, with the same stern secret to keep, and so near that the hem of their garments almost touched each other on the soft carpet. Hope felt a terrible hardness closing over her heart. What right had this cruel creature, with her fatal witcheries, to come between two persons who might have been so wholly happy? What sorrow would be saved, what shame, perhaps, be averted, should those sweet beguiling eyes never open, and that perfidious voice never deceive any more? Why tend the life of one who would leave the whole world happier, purer, freer, if she were dead?

In a tumult of thought, Hope went and sat half-unconsciously by the window. There was nothing to be seen except the steady beacon of the light-house and a pale-green glimmer, like an earthly star, from an anchored vessel. The night wind came softly in, soothing her with a touch like a mother's, in its grateful coolness. The air seemed full of half-vibrations, sub-noises, that crowded it as completely as do the insect sounds of midsummer; yet she could only distinguish the ripple beneath her feet, and the rote on the distant beach, and the busy wash of waters against every shore and islet of the bay. The mist was thick around her, but she knew that above it hung the sleepless stars, and the fancy came over her that perhaps the whole vast interval, from ocean up to sky, might be densely filled with the disembodied souls of her departed human kindred, waiting to see how she would endure that path of grief in which their steps had gone before. "It may be from this influence," she vaguely mused within herself, "that the ocean derives its endless song of sorrow. Perhaps we shall know the meaning when we understand that of the stars, and of our own sad lives."

She rose again and went to the bedside. It all seemed like a dream, and she was able to look at Emilia's existence and at her own and at all else, as if it were a great way off; as we watch the stars and know that no speculations of ours can reach those who there live or die untouched. Here beside her lay one who was dead, yet living, in her temporary trance, and to what would she wake, when it should end? This young creature had been sent into the world so fresh, so beautiful, so richly gifted; everything about her physical organization was so delicate and lovely; she had seemed like heliotrope, like a tube-rose in her purity and her passion (who was it said, "No heart is pure that is not passionate"?); and here was the end! Nothing external could have placed her where she was, no violence, no outrage, no evil of another's doing, could have reached her real life without her own consent; and now what kind of existence, what career, what possibility of happiness remained? Why could not God in his mercy take her, and give her to his holiest angels for schooling, ere it was yet too late?

Hope went and sat by the window once more. Her thoughts still clung heavily around one thought, as the white fog clung round the house. Where should she see any light? What opening for extrication, unless, indeed, Emilia should die? There could be no harm in that thought, for she knew it was not to be, and that the swoon would not last much longer. Who could devise anything? No one. There was nothing. Almost always in perplexities there is some thread by resolutely holding to which one escapes at last. Here there was none. There could probably be no concealment, certainly no explanation. In a few days John Lambert would return, and then the storm must break. He was probably a stern, jealous man, whose very dulness, once aroused, would be more formidable than if he had possessed keener perceptions.

Still her thoughts did not dwell on Philip. He was simply a part of that dull mass of pain that beset her and made her feel, as she had felt when drowning, that her heart had left her breast and nothing but will remained. She felt now, as then, the capacity to act with more than her accustomed resolution, though all that was within her seemed boiling up into her brain. As for Philip, all seemed a mere negation; there was a vacuum where his place had been. At most the thought of him came to her as some strange, vague thrill of added torture, penetrating her soul and then passing; just as ever and anon there came the sound of the fog-whistle on Brenton's Reef, miles away, piercing the dull air with its shrill and desolate wail, then dying into silence.

What a hopeless cloud lay upon them all forever,—upon Kate, upon Harry, upon their whole house! Then there was John Lambert; how could they keep it from him? how could they tell him? Who could predict what he would say? Would he take the worst and coarsest view of his young wife's mad action or the mildest? Would he be strong or weak; and what would be weakness, and what strength, in a position so strange? Would he put Emilia from him, send her out in the world desolate, her soul stained but by one wrong passion, yet with her reputation blighted as if there were no good in her? Could he be asked to shield and protect her, or what would become of her? She was legally a wife, and could only be separated from him through convicted shame.

Then, if separated, she could only marry Philip. Hope nerved herself to think of that, and it cost less effort than she expected.

There seemed a numbness on that side, instead of pain. But granting that he loved Emilia ever so deeply, was he a man to surrender his life and his ease and his fair name, in a hopeless effort to remove the ban that the world would place on her. Hope knew he would not; knew that even the simple-hearted and straightforward Harry would be far more capable of such heroism than the sentimental Malbone. Here the pang suddenly struck her; she was not so numb, after all!

As the leaves beside the window drooped motionless in the dank air, so her mind drooped into a settled depression. She pitied herself,—that lowest ebb of melancholy self-consciousness. She went back to Emilia, and, seating herself, studied every line of the girl's face, the soft texture of her hair, the veining of her eyelids. They were so lovely, she felt a sort of physical impulse to kiss them, as if they belonged to some utter stranger, whom she might be nursing in a hospital. Emilia looked as innocent as when Hope had tended her in the cradle. What is there, Hope thought, in sleep, in trance, and in death, that removes all harsh or disturbing impressions, and leaves only the most delicate and purest traits? Does the mind wander, and does an angel keep its place? Or is there really no sin but in thought, and are our sleeping thoughts incapable of sin? Perhaps even when we dream of doing wrong, the dream comes in a shape so lovely and misleading that we never recognize it for evil, and it makes no stain. Are our lives ever so pure as our dreams?

This thought somehow smote across her conscience, always so strong, and stirred it into a kind of spasm of introspection. "How selfish have I, too, been!" she thought. "I saw only what I wished to see, did only what I preferred. Loving Philip" (for the sudden self-reproach left her free to think of him), "I could not see that I was separating him from one whom he might perhaps have truly loved. If he made me blind, may he not easily have bewildered her, and have been himself bewildered? How I tried to force myself upon him, too! Ungenerous, unwomanly! What am I, that I should judge another?"

She threw herself on her knees at the bedside.

Still Emilia slept, but now she stirred her head in the slightest possible way, so that a single tress of silken hair slipped from its companions, and lay across her face. It was a faint sign that the trance was waning; the slight pressure disturbed her nerves, and her lips trembled once or twice, as if to relieve themselves of the soft annoyance. Hope watched her in a vague, distant way, took note of the minutest motion, yet as if some vast weight hung upon her own limbs and made all interference impossible. Still there was a fascination of sympathy in dwelling on that atom of discomfort, that tiny suffering, which she alone could remove. The very vastness of this tragedy that hung about the house made it an inexpressible relief to her to turn and concentrate her thoughts for a moment on this slight distress, so easily ended.

Strange, by what slender threads our lives are knitted to each other! Here was one who had taken Hope's whole existence in her hands, crushed it, and thrown it away. Hope had soberly said to herself, just before, that death would be better than life for her young sister. Yet now it moved her beyond endurance to see that fair form troubled, even while unconscious, by a feather's weight of pain; and all the lifelong habit of tenderness resumed in a moment its sway.

She approached her fingers to the offending tress, very slowly, half withholding them at the very last, as if the touch would burn her. She was almost surprised that it did not. She looked to see if it did not hurt Emilia. But it now seemed as if the slumbering girl enjoyed the caressing contact of the smooth fingers, and turned her head, almost imperceptibly, to meet them. This was more than Hope could bear. It was as if that slight motion were a puncture to relieve her overburdened heart; a thousand thoughts swept over her,—of their father, of her sister's childhood, of her years of absent expectation; she thought how young the girl was, how fascinating, how passionate, how tempted; all this swept across her in a great wave of nervous reaction, and when Emilia returned to consciousness, she was lying in her sister's arms, her face bathed in Hope's tears.

XIX. DE PROFUNDIS.

THIS was the history of Emilia's concealed visits to Malbone.

One week after her marriage, in a crisis of agony, Emilia took up her pen, dipped it in fire, and wrote thus to him:—

"Philip Malbone, why did nobody ever tell me what marriage is where there is no love? This man who calls himself my husband is no worse, I suppose, than other men. It is only for being what is called by that name that I abhor him. Good God! what am I to do? It was not for money that I married him,—that you know very well; I cared no more for his money than for himself. I thought it was the only way to save Hope. She has been very good to me, and perhaps I should love her, if I could love anybody. Now I have done what will only make more misery, for I cannot bear it. Philip, I am alone in this wide world, except for you. Tell me what to do. I will haunt you till you die, unless you tell me. Answer this, or I will write again."

Terrified by this letter, absolutely powerless to guide the life with which he had so desperately entangled himself, Philip let one day pass without answering, and that evening he found Emilia at his door, she having glided unnoticed up the main stairway. She was so excited, it was equally dangerous to send her away or to admit her, and he drew her in, darkening the windows and locking the door. On the whole, it was not so bad as he expected; at least, there was less violence and more despair. She covered her face with her hands, and writhed in anguish, when she said that she had utterly degraded herself by this loveless marriage. She scarcely mentioned her husband. She made no complaint of him, and even spoke of him as generous. It seemed as if this made it worse, and as if she would be happier if she could expend herself in hating him. She spoke of him rather as a mere witness to some shame for which she herself was responsible; bearing him no malice, but tortured by the thought that he should exist.

Then she turned on Malbone. "Philip, why did you ever interfere with my life? I should have been very happy with Antoine if you had let me marry him, for I never should have known what it was to love you. Oh! I wish he were here now, even he,—any one who loved me truly, and whom I could love only a little. I would go away with such a person anywhere, and never trouble you and Hope any more. What shall I do? Philip, you might tell me what to do. Once you told me always to come to you."

"What can you do?" he asked gloomily, in return.

"I cannot imagine," she said, with a desolate look, more pitiable than passion, on her young face. "I wish to save Hope, and to save my—to save Mr. Lambert. Philip, you do not love me. I do not call it love. There is no passion in your veins; it is only a sort of sympathetic selfishness. Hope is infinitely better than you are, and I believe she is more capable of loving. I began by hating her, but if she loves you as I think she does, she has treated me more generously than ever one woman treated another. For she could not look at me and not know that I loved you. I did love you. O Philip, tell me what to do!"

Such beauty in anguish, the thrill of the possession of such love, the possibility of soothing by tenderness the wild mood which he could not meet by counsel,—it would have taken a stronger or less sympathetic nature than Malbone's to endure all this. It swept him away; this revival of passion was irresistible. When her pent-up feeling was once uttered, she turned to his love as a fancied salvation. It was a terrible remedy. She had never looked more beautiful, and yet she seemed to have grown old at once; her very caresses appeared to burn. She lingered and lingered, and still he kept her there; and when it was no longer possible for her to go without disturbing the house, he led her to a secret spiral stairway, which went from attic to cellar of that stately old mansion, and which opened by one or more doors on each landing, as his keen eye had found out. Descending this, he went forth with her into the dark and silent night. The mist hung around the house; the wet leaves fluttered and fell upon their cheeks; the water lapped desolately against the pier. Philip found a carriage and sent her back to Mrs. Meredith's, where she was staying during the brief absence of John Lambert.

These concealed meetings, once begun, became an absorbing excitement. She came several times, staying half an hour, an hour, two hours. They were together long enough for suffering, never long enough for soothing. It was a poor substitute for happiness. Each time she came, Malbone wished that she might never go or never return. His warier nature was feverish with solicitude and with self-reproach; he liked the excitement of slight risks, but this was far too intense, the vibrations too extreme. She, on the other hand, rode triumphant over waves of passion which cowed him. He dared not exclude her; he dared not continue to admit her; he dared not free himself; he could not be happy. The privacy of the concealed stairway saved them from outward dangers, but not from inward fears. Their interviews were first blissful, then anxious, then sad, then stormy. It was at the end of such a storm that Emilia had passed into one of those deathly calms which belonged to her physical temperament; and it was under these circumstances that Hope had followed Philip to the door.

XX. AUNT JANE TO THE RESCUE.

THE thing that saves us from insanity during great grief is that there is usually something to do, and the mind composes itself to the mechanical task of adjusting the details. Hope dared not look forward an inch into the future; that way madness lay. Fortunately, it was plain what must come first,—to keep the whole thing within their own walls, and therefore to make some explanation to Mrs. Meredith, whose servants had doubtless been kept up all night awaiting Emilia. Profoundly perplexed what to say or not to say to her, Hope longed with her whole soul for an adviser. Harry and Kate were both away, and besides, she shrank from darkening their young lives as hers had been darkened. She resolved to seek counsel in the one person who most thoroughly distrusted Emilia,—Aunt Jane.

This lady was in a particularly happy mood that day. Emilia, who did all kinds of fine needle-work exquisitely, had just embroidered for Aunt Jane some pillow-cases. The original suggestion came from Hope, but it never cost Emilia anything to keep a secret, and she had presented the gift very sweetly, as if it were a thought of her own. Aunt Jane, who with all her penetration as to facts was often very guileless as to motives, was thoroughly touched by the humility and the embroidery.

"All last night," she said, "I kept waking up, and thinking about Christian charity and my pillow-cases."

It was, therefore, a very favorable day for Hope's consultation, though it was nearly noon before her aunt was visible, perhaps because it took so long to make up her bed with the new adornments.

Hope said frankly to Aunt Jane that there were some circumstances about which she should rather not be questioned, but that Emilia had come there the previous night from the ball, had been seized with one of her peculiar attacks, and had stayed all night. Aunt Jane kept her eyes steadily fixed on Hope's sad face, and, when the tale was ended, drew her down and kissed her lips.

"Now tell me, dear," she said; "what comes first?"

"The first thing is," said Hope, "to have Emilia's absence explained to Mrs. Meredith in some such way that she will think no more of it, and not talk about it."

"Certainly," said Aunt Jane. "There is but one way to do that. I will call on her myself."

"You, auntie?" said Hope.

"Yes, I," said her aunt. "I have owed her a call for five years. It is the only thing that will excite her so much as to put all else out of her head."

"O auntie!" said Hope, greatly relieved, "if you only would! But ought you really to go out? It is almost raining."

"I shall go," said Aunt Jane, decisively, "if it rains little boys!"

"But will not Mrs. Meredith wonder—?" began Hope.

"That is one advantage," interrupted her aunt, "of being an absurd old woman. Nobody ever wonders at anything I do, or else it is that they never stop wondering."

She sent Ruth erelong to order the horses. Hope collected her various wrappers, and Ruth, returning, got her mistress into a state of preparation.

"If I might say one thing more," Hope whispered.

"Certainly," said her aunt. "Ruth, go to my chamber, and get me a pin."

"What kind of a pin, ma'am?" asked that meek handmaiden, from the doorway.

"What a question!" said her indignant mistress. "Any kind. The common pin of North America. Now, Hope?" as the door closed.

"I think it better, auntie," said Hope, "that Philip should not stay here longer at present. You can truly say that the house is full, and—"

"I have just had a note from him," said Aunt Jane severely. "He has gone to lodge at the hotel. What next?"

"Aunt Jane," said Hope, looking her full in the face, "I have not the slightest idea what to do next."

("The next thing for me," thought her aunt, "is to have a little plain speech with that misguided child upstairs.")

"I can see no way out," pursued Hope.

"Darling!" said Aunt Jane, with a voice full of womanly sweetness, "there is always a way out, or else the world would have stopped long ago. Perhaps it would have been better if it had stopped, but you see it has not. All we can do is, to live on and try our best."

She bade Hope leave Emilia to her, and furthermore stipulated that Hope should go to her pupils as usual, that afternoon, as it was their last lesson. The young girl shrank from the effort, but the elder lady was inflexible. She had her own purpose in it. Hope once out of the way, Aunt Jane could deal with Emilia.

No human being, when met face to face with Aunt Jane, had ever failed to yield up to her the whole truth she sought. Emilia was on that day no exception. She was prostrate, languid, humble, denied nothing, was ready to concede every point but one. Never, while she lived, would she dwell beneath John Lambert's roof again. She had left it impulsively, she admitted, scarce knowing what she did. But she would never return there to live. She would go once more and see that all was in order for Mr. Lambert, both in the house and on board the yacht, where they were to have taken up their abode for a time. There were new servants in the house, a new captain on the yacht; she would trust Mr. Lambert's comfort to none of them; she would do her full duty. Duty! the more utterly she felt herself to be gliding away from him forever, the more pains she was ready to lavish in doing these nothings well. About every insignificant article he owned she seemed to feel the most scrupulous and wife-like responsibility; while she yet knew that all she had was to him nothing, compared with the possession of herself; and it was the thought of this last ownership that drove her to despair.

Sweet and plaintive as the child's face was, it had a glimmer of wildness and a hunted look, that baffled Aunt Jane a little, and compelled her to temporize. She consented that Emilia should go to her own house, on condition that she would not see Philip,—which was readily and even eagerly promised,—and that Hope should spend the night with Emilia, which proposal was ardently accepted.

It occurred to Aunt Jane that nothing better could happen than for John Lambert, on returning, to find his wife at home; and to secure this result, if possible, she telegraphed to him to come at once.

Meantime Hope gave her inevitable music-lesson, so absorbed in her own thoughts that it was all as mechanical as the metronome. As she came out upon the Avenue for the walk home, she saw a group of people from a gardener's house, who had collected beside a muddy crossing, where a team of cart-horses had refused to stir. Presently they sprang forward with a great jerk, and a little Irish child was thrown beneath the wheel. Hope sprang forward to grasp the child, and the wheel struck her also; but she escaped with a dress torn and smeared, while the cart passed over the little girl's arm, breaking it in two places. She screamed and then grew faint, as Hope lifted her. The mother received the burden with a wail of anguish; the other Irishwomen pressed around her with the dense and suffocating sympathy of their nation. Hope bade one and another run for a physician, but nobody stirred. There was no surgical aid within a mile or more. Hope looked round in despair, then glanced at her own disordered garments.

"As sure as you live!" shouted a well-known voice from a carriage which had stopped behind them. "If that isn't Hope what's-her-name, wish I may never! Here's a lark! Let me come there!" And the speaker pushed through the crowd.

"Miss Ingleside," said Hope, decisively, "this child's arm is broken. There is nobody to go for a physician. Except for the condition I am in, I would ask you to take me there at once in your carriage; but as it is—"

"As it is, I must ask you, hey?" said Blanche, finishing the sentence. "Of course. No mistake. Sans dire. Jones, junior, this lady will join us. Don't look so scared, man. Are you anxious about your cushions or your reputation?"

The youth simpered and disclaimed.

"Jump in, then, Miss Maxwell. Never mind the expense. It's only the family carriage;—surname and arms of Jones. Lucky there are no parents to the fore. Put my shawl over you, so."

"O Blanche!" said Hope, "what injustice—"

"I've done myself?" said the volatile damsel. "Not a doubt of it. That's my style, you know. But I have some sense; I know who's who. Now, Jones, junior, make your man handle the ribbons. I've always had a grudge against that ordinance about fast driving, and now's our chance."

And the sacred "ordinance," with all other proprieties, was left in ruins that day. They tore along the Avenue with unexplained and most inexplicable speed, Hope being concealed by riding backward, and by a large shawl, and Blanche and her admirer receiving the full indignation of every chaste and venerable eye. Those who had tolerated all this girl's previous improprieties were obliged to admit that the line must be drawn somewhere. She at once lost several good invitations and a matrimonial offer, since Jones, junior, was swept away by his parents to be wedded without delay to a consumptive heiress who had long pined for his whiskers; and Count Posen, in his Souvenirs, was severer on Blanche's one good deed than on the worst of her follies.

A few years after, when Blanche, then the fearless wife of a regular-army officer, was helping Hope in the hospitals at Norfolk, she would stop to shout with delight over the reminiscence of that stately Jones equipage in mad career, amid the barking of dogs and the groaning of dowagers. "After all, Hope," she would say, "the fastest thing I ever did was under your orders."

XXI. A STORM.

THE members of the household were all at the window about noon, next day, watching the rise of a storm. A murky wing of cloud, shaped like a hawk's, hung over the low western hills across the bay. Then the hawk became an eagle, and the eagle a gigantic phantom, that hovered over half the visible sky. Beneath it, a little scud of vapor, moved by some cross-current of air, raced rapidly against the wind, just above the horizon, like smoke from a battle-field.

As the cloud ascended, the water grew rapidly blacker, and in half an hour broke into jets of white foam, all over its surface, with an angry look. Meantime a white film of fog spread down the bay from the northward. The wind hauled from southwest to northwest, so suddenly and strongly that all the anchored boats seemed to have swung round instantaneously, without visible process. The instant the wind shifted, the rain broke forth, filling the air in a moment with its volume, and cutting so sharply that it seemed like hail, though no hailstones reached the ground. At the same time there rose upon the water a dense white film, which seemed to grow together from a hundred different directions, and was made partly of rain, and partly of the blown edges of the spray. There was but a glimpse of this; for in a few moments it was impossible to see two rods; but when the first gust was over, the water showed itself again, the jets of spray all beaten down, and regular waves, of dull lead-color, breaking higher on the shore. All the depth of blackness had left the sky, and there remained only an obscure and ominous gray, through which the lightning flashed white, not red. Boats came driving in from the mouth of the bay with a rag of sail up; the men got them moored with difficulty, and when they sculled ashore in the skiffs, a dozen comrades stood ready to grasp and haul them in. Others launched skiffs in sheltered places, and pulled out bareheaded to bail out their fishing-boats and keep them from swamping at their moorings.

The shore was thronged with men in oilskin clothes and by women with shawls over their heads. Aunt Jane, who always felt responsible for whatever went on in the elements, sat in-doors with one lid closed, wincing at every flash, and watching the universe with the air of a coachman guiding six wild horses.

Just after the storm had passed its height, two veritable wild horses were reined up at the door, and Philip burst in, his usual self-composure gone.

"Emilia is out sailing!" he exclaimed,—"alone with Lambert's boatman, in this gale. They say she was bound for Narragansett."

"Impossible!" cried Hope, turning pale. "I left her not three hours ago." Then she remembered that Emilia had spoken of going on board the yacht, to superintend some arrangements, but had said no more about it, when she opposed it.

"Harry!" said Aunt Jane, quickly, from her chair by the window, "see that fisherman. He has just come ashore and is telling something. Ask him."

The fisherman had indeed seen Lambert's boat, which was well known. Something seemed to be the matter with the sail, but before the storm struck her, it had been hauled down. They must have taken in water enough, as it was. He had himself been obliged to bail out three times, running in from the reef.

"Was there any landing which they could reach?" Harry asked.

There was none,—but the light-ship lay right in their track, and if they had good luck, they might get aboard of her.

"The boatman?" said Philip, anxiously,—"Mr. Lambert's boatman; is he a good sailor?"

"Don't know," was the reply. "Stranger here. Dutchman, Frenchman, Portegee, or some kind of a foreigner."

"Seems to understand himself in a boat," said another.

"Mr. Malbone knows him," said a third. "The same that dove with the young woman under the steamboat paddles."

"Good grit," said the first.

"That's so," was the answer. "But grit don't teach a man the channel."

All agreed to this axiom; but as there was so strong a probability that the voyagers had reached the light-ship, there seemed less cause for fear.

The next question was, whether it was possible to follow them. All agreed that it would be foolish for any boat to attempt it, till the wind had blown itself out, which might be within half an hour. After that, some predicted a calm, some a fog, some a renewal of the storm; there was the usual variety of opinions. At any rate, there might perhaps be an interval during which they could go out, if the gentlemen did not mind a wet jacket.

Within the half-hour came indeed an interval of calm, and a light shone behind the clouds from the west. It faded soon into a gray fog, with puffs of wind from the southwest again. When the young men went out with the boatmen, the water had grown more quiet, save where angry little gusts ruffled it. But these gusts made it necessary to carry a double reef, and they made but little progress against wind and tide.

A dark-gray fog, broken by frequent wind-flaws, makes the ugliest of all days on the water. A still, pale fog is soothing; it lulls nature to a kind of repose. But a windy fog with occasional sunbeams and sudden films of metallic blue breaking the leaden water,—this carries an impression of something weird and treacherous in the universe, and suggests caution.

As the boat floated on, every sight and sound appeared strange. The music from the fort came sudden and startling through the vaporous eddies. A tall white schooner rose instantaneously near them, like a light-house. They could see the steam of the factory floating low, seeking some outlet between cloud and water. As they drifted past a wharf, the great black piles of coal hung high and gloomy; then a stray sunbeam brought out their peacock colors; then came the fog again, driving hurriedly by, as if impatient to go somewhere and enraged at the obstacle. It seemed to have a vast inorganic life of its own, a volition and a whim. It drew itself across the horizon like a curtain; then advanced in trampling armies up the bay; then marched in masses northward; then suddenly grew thin, and showed great spaces of sunlight; then drifted across the low islands, like long tufts of wool; then rolled itself away toward the horizon; then closed in again, pitiless and gray.

Suddenly something vast towered amid the mist above them. It was the French war-ship returned to her anchorage once more, and seeming in that dim atmosphere to be something spectral and strange that had taken form out of the elements. The muzzles of great guns rose tier above tier, along her side; great boats hung one above another, on successive pairs of davits, at her stern. So high was her hull, that the topmost boat and the topmost gun appeared to be suspended in middle air; and yet this was but the beginning of her altitude. Above these were the heavy masts, seen dimly through the mist; between these were spread eight dark lines of sailors' clothes, which, with the massive yards above, looked like part of some ponderous framework built to reach the sky. This prolongation of the whole dark mass toward the heavens had a portentous look to those who gazed from below; and when the denser fog sometimes furled itself away from the topgallant masts, hitherto invisible, and showed them rising loftier yet, and the tricolor at the mizzen-mast-head looking down as if from the zenith, then they all seemed to appertain to something of more than human workmanship; a hundred wild tales of phantom vessels came up to the imagination, and it was as if that one gigantic structure were expanding to fill all space from sky to sea.

They were swept past it; the fog closed in; it was necessary to land near the Fort, and proceed on foot. They walked across the rough peninsula, while the mist began to disperse again, and they were buoyant with expectation. As they toiled onward, the fog suddenly met them at the turn of a lane where it had awaited them, like an enemy. As they passed into those gray and impalpable arms, the whole world changed again.

They walked toward the sound of the sea. As they approached it, the dull hue that lay upon it resembled that of the leaden sky. The two elements could hardly be distinguished except as the white outlines of the successive breakers were lifted through the fog. The lines of surf appeared constantly to multiply upon the beach, and yet, on counting them, there were never any more. Sometimes, in the distance, masses of foam rose up like a wall where the horizon ought to be; and, as the coming waves took form out of the unseen, it seemed as if no phantom were too vast or shapeless to come rolling in upon their dusky shoulders.

Presently a frail gleam of something like the ghost of dead sunshine made them look toward the west. Above the dim roofs of Castle Hill mansion-house, the sinking sun showed luridly through two rifts of cloud, and then the swift motion of the nearer vapor veiled both sun and cloud, and banished them into almost equal remoteness.

Leaving the beach on their right, and passing the high rocks of the Pirate's Cave, they presently descended to the water's edge once more. The cliffs rose to a distorted height in the dimness; sprays of withered grass nodded along the edge, like Ossian's spectres. Light seemed to be vanishing from the universe, leaving them alone with the sea. And when a solitary loon uttered his wild cry, and rising, sped away into the distance, it was as if life were following light into an equal annihilation. That sense of vague terror, with which the ocean sometimes controls the fancy, began to lay its grasp on them. They remembered that Emilia, in speaking once of her intense shrinking from death, had said that the sea was the only thing from which she would not fear to meet it.

Fog exaggerates both for eye and ear; it is always a sounding-board for the billows; and in this case, as often happens, the roar did not appear to proceed from the waves themselves, but from some source in the unseen horizon, as if the spectators were shut within a beleaguered fortress, and this thundering noise came from an impetuous enemy outside. Ever and anon there was a distinct crash of heavier sound, as if some special barricade had at length been beaten in, and the garrison must look to their inner defences.

The tide was unusually high, and scarcely receded with the ebb, though the surf increased; the waves came in with constant rush and wail, and with an ominous rattle of pebbles on the little beaches, beneath the powerful suction of the undertow; and there were more and more of those muffled throbs along the shore which tell of coming danger as plainly as minute-guns. With these came mingled that yet more inexplicable humming which one hears at intervals in such times, like strains of music caught and tangled in the currents of stormy air,—strains which were perhaps the filmy thread on which tales of sirens and mermaids were first strung, and in which, at this time, they would fain recognize the voice of Emilia.

XXII. OUT OF THE DEPTHS.

AS the night closed in, the wind rose steadily, still blowing from the southwest. In Brenton's kitchen they found a group round a great fire of driftwood; some of these were fishermen who had with difficulty made a landing on the beach, and who confirmed the accounts already given. The boat had been seen sailing for the Narragansett shore, and when the squall came, the boatman had lowered and reefed the sail, and stood for the light-ship. They must be on board of her, if anywhere.

"There are safe there?" asked Philip, eagerly.

"Only place where they would be safe, then," said the spokesman.

"Unless the light-ship parts," said an old fellow.

"Parts!" said the other. "Sixty fathom of two-inch chain, and old Joe talks about parting."

"Foolish, of course," said Philip; "but it's a dangerous shore."

"That's so," was the answer. "Never saw so many lines of reef show outside, neither."

"There's an old saying on this shore," said Joe:—

> "When Price's Neck goes to Brenton's Reef,
> Body and soul will come to grief.
> But when Brenton's Reef comes to Price's Neck,
> Soul and body are both a wreck."

"What does it mean?" asked Harry.

"It only means," said somebody, "that when you see it white all the way out from the Neck to the Reef, you can't take the inside passage."

"But what does the last half mean?" persisted Harry.

"Don't know as I know," said the veteran, and relapsed into silence, in which all joined him, while the wind howled and whistled outside, and the barred windows shook.

Weary and restless with vain waiting, they looked from the doorway at the weather. The door went back with a slam, and the gust swooped down on them with that special blast that always seems to linger just outside on such nights, ready for the first head that shows itself. They closed the door upon the flickering fire and the uncouth shadows within, and went forth into the night. At first the solid blackness seemed to lay a weight on their foreheads. There was absolutely nothing to be seen but the two lights of the light-ship, glaring from the dark sea like a wolf's eyes from a cavern. They looked nearer and brighter than in ordinary nights, and appeared to the excited senses of the young men to dance strangely on the waves, and to be always opposite to them, as they moved along the shore with the wind almost at their backs.

"What did that old fellow mean?" said Malbone in Harry's ear, as they came to a protected place and could hear each other, "by talking of Brenton's Reef coming to Price's Neck."

"Some sailor's doggerel," said Harry, indifferently. "Here is Price's Neck before us, and yonder is Brenton's Reef."

"Where?" said Philip, looking round bewildered.

The lights had gone, as if the wolf, weary of watching, had suddenly closed his eyes, and slumbered in his cave.

Harry trembled and shivered. In Heaven's name, what could this disappearance mean?

Suddenly a sheet of lightning came, so white and intense, it sent its light all the way out to the horizon and exhibited far-off vessels, that reeled and tossed and looked as if wandering without a guide. But this was not so startling as what it showed in the foreground.

There drifted heavily upon the waves, within full view from the shore, moving parallel to it, yet gradually approaching, an uncouth shape that seemed a vessel and yet not a vessel; two stunted masts projected above, and below there could be read, in dark letters that apparently swayed and trembled in the wan lightning, as the thing moved on,

BRENTON'S REEF.

Philip, leaning against a rock, gazed into the darkness where the apparition had been; even Harry felt a thrill of half-superstitious wonder, and listened half mechanically to a rough sailor's voice at his ear:—

"God! old Joe was right. There's one wreck that is bound to make many. The light-ship has parted."

"Drifting ashore," said Harry, his accustomed clearness of head coming back at a flash. "Where will she strike?"

"Price's Neck," said the sailor.

Harry turned to Philip and spoke to him, shouting in his ear the explanation. Malbone's lips moved mechanically, but he said nothing. Passively, he let Harry take him by the arm, and lead him on.

Following the sailor, they rounded a projecting point, and found themselves a little sheltered from the wind. Not knowing the region, they stumbled about among the rocks, and scarcely knew when they neared the surf, except when a wave came swashing round their very feet. Pausing at the end of a cove, they stood beside their conductor, and their eyes, now grown accustomed, could make out vaguely the outlines of the waves.

The throat of the cove was so shoal and narrow, and the mass of the waves so great, that they reared their heads enormously, just outside, and spending their strength there, left a lower level within the cove. Yet sometimes a series of great billows would come straight on, heading directly for the entrance, and then the surface of the water within was seen to swell suddenly upward as if by a terrible inward magic of its own; it rose and rose, as if it would ingulf everything; then as rapidly sank, and again presented a mere quiet vestibule before the excluded waves.

They saw in glimpses, as the lightning flashed, the shingly beach, covered with a mass of creamy foam, all tremulous and fluctuating in the wind; and this foam was constantly torn away by the gale in great shreds, that whirled by them as if the very fragments of the ocean were fleeing from it in terror, to take refuge in the less frightful element of air.

Still the wild waves reared their heads, like savage, crested animals, now white, now black, looking in from the entrance of the cove. And now there silently drifted upon them something higher, vaster, darker than themselves,—the doomed vessel. It was strange how slowly and steadily she swept in,—for her broken chain-cable dragged, as it afterwards proved, and kept her stern-on to the shore,—and they could sometimes hear amid the tumult a groan that seemed to come from the very heart of the earth, as she painfully drew her keel over hidden reefs. Over five of these (as was afterwards found) she had already drifted, and she rose and fell more than once on the high waves at the very mouth of the cove, like a wild bird hovering ere it pounces.

Then there came one of those great confluences of waves described already, which, lifting her bodily upward, higher and higher and higher, suddenly rushed with her into the basin, filling it like an opened dry-dock, crashing and roaring round the vessel and upon the rocks, then sweeping out again and leaving her lodged, still stately and steady, at the centre of the cove.

They could hear from the crew a mingled sound, that came as a shout of excitement from some and a shriek of despair from others. The vivid lightning revealed for a moment those on shipboard to those on shore; and blinding as it was, it lasted long enough to show figures gesticulating and pointing. The old sailor, Mitchell, tried to build a fire among the rocks nearest the vessel, but it was impossible, because of the wind. This was a disappointment, for the light would have taken away half the danger, and more than half the terror. Though the cove was more quiet than the ocean, yet it was fearful enough, even there. The vessel might hold together till morning, but who could tell? It was almost certain that those on board would try to land, and there was nothing to do but to await the effort. The men from the farmhouse had meanwhile come down with ropes.

It was simply impossible to judge with any accuracy of the distance of the ship. One of these new-comers, who declared that she was lodged very near, went to a point of rocks, and shouted to those on board to heave him a rope. The tempest suppressed his voice, as it had put out the fire. But perhaps the lightning had showed him to the dark figures on the stern; for when the next flash came, they saw a rope flung, which fell short. The real distance was more than a hundred yards.

Then there was a long interval of darkness. The moment the next flash came they saw a figure let down by a rope from the stern of the vessel, while the hungry waves reared like wolves to seize it. Everybody crowded down to the nearest rocks, looking this way and that for a head to appear. They pressed eagerly in every direction where a bit of plank or a barrel-head floated; they fancied faint cries here and there, and went aimlessly to and fro. A new effort, after half a dozen failures, sent a blaze mounting up fitfully among the rocks, startling all with the sudden change its blessed splendor made. Then a shrill shout from one of the watchers summoned all to a cleft in the cove, half shaded from the firelight, where there came rolling in amidst the surf, more dead than alive, the body of a man. He was the young foreigner, John Lambert's boatman. He bore still around him the rope that was to save the rest.

How pale and eager their faces looked as they bent above him! But the eagerness was all gone from his, and only the pallor left. While the fishermen got the tackle rigged, such as it was, to complete the communication with the vessel, the young men worked upon the boatman, and soon had him restored to consciousness. He was able to explain that the ship had been severely strained, and that all on board believed she would go to pieces before morning. No one would risk being the first to take the water, and he had at last volunteered, as being the best swimmer, on condition that Emilia should be next sent, when the communication was established.

Two ropes were then hauled on board the vessel, a larger and a smaller. By the flickering firelight and the rarer flashes of lightning (the rain now falling in torrents) they saw a hammock slung to the larger rope; a woman's form was swathed in it; and the smaller rope being made fast to this, they found by pulling that she could be drawn towards the shore. Those on board steadied the hammock as it was lowered from the ship, but the waves seemed maddened by this effort to escape their might, and they leaped up at her again and again. The rope dropped beneath her weight, and all that could be done from shore was to haul her in as fast as possible, to abbreviate the period of buffeting and suffocation. As she neared the rocks she could be kept more safe from the water; faster and faster she was drawn in; sometimes there came some hitch and stoppage, but by steady patience it was overcome.

She was so near the rocks that hands were already stretched to grasp her, when there came one of the great surging waves that sometimes filled the basin. It gave a terrible lurch to the stranded vessel hitherto so erect; the larger rope snapped instantly; the guiding rope was twitched from the hands that held it; and the canvas that held Emilia was caught and swept away like a shred of foam, and lost amid the whiteness of the seething froth below. Fifteen minutes after, the hammock came ashore empty, the lashings having parted.

The cold daybreak was just opening, though the wind still blew keenly, when they found the body of Emilia. It was swathed in a roll of sea-weed, lying in the edge of the surf, on a broad, flat rock near where the young boatman had come ashore. The face was not disfigured; the clothing was only torn a little, and tangled closely round her; but the life was gone.

It was Philip who first saw her; and he stood beside her for a moment motionless, stunned into an aspect of tranquility. This, then, was the end. All his ready sympathy, his wooing tenderness, his winning compliances, his self-indulgent softness, his perilous amiability, his reluctance to give pain or to see sorrow,—all had ended in this. For once, he must force even his accommodating and evasive nature to meet the plain, blank truth. Now all his characteristics appeared changed by the encounter; it was Harry who was ready, thoughtful, attentive,—while Philip, who usually had all these traits, was paralyzed among his dreams. Could he have fancied such a scene beforehand, he would have vowed that no hand but his should touch the breathless form of Emilia. As it was, he instinctively made way for the quick gathering of the others, as if almost any one else had a better right to be there.

The storm had blown itself out by sunrise; the wind had shifted, beating down the waves; it seemed as if everything in nature were exhausted. The very tide had ebbed away. The light-ship rested between the rocks, helpless, still at the mercy of the returning waves, and yet still upright and with that stately look of unconscious pleading which all shipwrecked vessels wear, it is wonderfully like the look I have seen in the face of some dead soldier, on whom war had done its worst. Every line of a ship is so built for motion, every part, while afloat, seems so full of life and so answering to the human life it bears, that this paralysis of shipwreck touches the imagination as if the motionless thing had once been animated by a soul.

And not far from the vessel, in a chamber of the seaside farm-house, lay the tenderer and fairer wreck of Emilia. Her storms and her passions were ended. The censure of the world, the anguish of friends, the clinging arms of love, were nothing now to her. Again the soft shelter of unconsciousness had clasped her in; but this time the trance was longer and the faintness was unto death.

From the moment of her drifting ashore, it was the young boatman who had assumed the right to care for her and to direct everything. Philip seemed stunned; Harry was his usual clear-headed and efficient self; but to his honest eyes much revealed itself in a little while; and when Hope arrived in the early morning, he said to her, "This boatman, who once saved your life, is Emilia's Swiss lover, Antoine Marval."

"More than lover," said the young Swiss, overhearing. "She was my wife before God, when you took her from me. In my country, a betrothal is as sacred as a marriage. Then came that man, he filled her heart with illusions, and took her away in my absence. When my brother was here in the corvette, he found her for me. Then I came for her; I saved her sister; then I saw the name on the card and would not give my own. I became her servant. She saw me in the yacht, only once; she knew me; she was afraid. Then she said, 'Perhaps I still love you,—a little; I do not know; I am in despair; take me from this home I hate.' We sailed that day in the small boat for Narragansett,—I know not where. She hardly looked up or spoke; but for me, I cared for nothing since she was with me. When the storm came, she was frightened, and said, 'It is a retribution.' I said, 'You shall never go back.' She never did. Here she is. You cannot take her from me."

Once on board the light-ship, she had been assigned the captain's state-room, while Antoine watched at the door. She seemed to shrink from him whenever he went to speak to her, he owned, but she answered kindly and gently, begging to be left alone. When at last the vessel parted her moorings, he persuaded Emilia to come on deck and be lashed to the mast, where she sat without complaint.

Who can fathom the thoughts of that bewildered child, as she sat amid the spray and the howling of the blast, while the doomed vessel drifted on with her to the shore? Did all the error and sorrow of her life pass distinctly before her? Or did the roar of the surf lull her into quiet, like the unconscious kindness of wild creatures that toss and bewilder their prey into unconsciousness ere they harm it? None can tell. Death answers no questions; it only makes them needless.

The morning brought to the scene John Lambert, just arrived by land from New York.

The passion of John Lambert for his wife was of that kind which ennobles while it lasts, but which rarely outlasts marriage. A man of such uncongenial mould will love an enchanting woman with a mad, absorbing passion, where self-sacrifice is so mingled with selfishness that the two emotions seem one; he will hungrily yearn to possess her, to call her by his own name, to hold her in his arms, to kill any one else who claims her. But when she is once his wife, and his arms hold a body without a soul,—no soul at least for him,—then her image is almost inevitably profaned, and the passion which began too high for earth ends far too low for heaven. Let now death change that form to marble, and instantly it resumes its virgin holiness; though the presence of life did not sanctify, its departure does. It is only the true lover to whom the breathing form is as sacred as the breathless.

That ideality of nature which love had developed in this man, and which had already drooped a little during his brief period of marriage, was born again by the side of death. While Philip wandered off silent and lonely with his grief, John Lambert knelt by the beautiful remains, talking inarticulately, his eyes streaming with unchecked tears. Again was Emilia, in her marble paleness, the calm centre of a tragedy she herself had caused. The wild, ungoverned child was the image of peace; it was the stolid and prosperous man who was in the storm. It was not till Hope came that there was any change. Then his prostrate nature sought hers, as the needle leaps to the iron; the first touch of her hand, the sight of her kiss upon Emilia's forehead, made him strong. It was the thorough subjection of a worldly man to the higher organization of a noble woman, and thenceforth it never varied. In later years, after he had foolishly sought, as men will, to win her to a nearer tie, there was no moment when she had not full control over his time, his energies, and his wealth.

After it was all ended, Hope told him everything that had happened; but in that wild moment of his despair she told him nothing. Only she and Harry knew the story of the young Swiss; and now that Emilia was gone, her early lover had no wish to speak of her to any but these two, or to linger long where she had been doubly lost to him, by marriage and by death. The world, with all its prying curiosity, usually misses the key to the very incidents about which it asks most questions; and of the many who gossiped or mourned concerning Emilia, none knew the tragic complication which her death alone could have solved. The breaking of Hope's engagement to Philip was attributed to every cause but the true one. And when the storm of the great Rebellion broke over the land, its vast calamity absorbed all minor griefs.

XXIII. REQUIESCAT.

THANK God! it is not within the power of one man's errors to blight the promise of a life like that of Hope. It is but a feeble destiny that is wrecked by passion, when it should be ennobled. Aunt Jane and Kate watched Hope closely during her years of probation, for although she fancied herself to be keeping her own counsel, yet her career lay in broad light for them. She was like yonder sailboat, which floats conspicuous by night amid the path of moonbeams, and which yet seems to its own voyagers to be remote and unseen upon a waste of waves.

Why should I linger over the details of her life, after the width of ocean lay between her and Malbone, and a manhood of self-denying usefulness had begun to show that even he could learn something by life's retributions? We know what she was, and it is of secondary importance where she went or what she did. Kindle the light of the light-house, and it has nothing to do, except to shine. There is for it no wrong direction. There is no need to ask, "How? Over which especial track of distant water must my light go forth, to find the wandering vessel to be guided in?" It simply shines. Somewhere there is a ship that needs it, or if not, the light does its duty. So did Hope.

We must leave her here. Yet I cannot bear to think of her as passing through earthly life without tasting its deepest bliss, without the last pure ecstasy of human love, without the kisses of her own children on her lips, their waxen fingers on her bosom.

And yet again, is this life so long? May it not be better to wait until its little day is done, and the summer night of old age has yielded to a new morning, before attaining that acme of joy? Are there enough successive grades of bliss for all eternity, if so much be consummated here? Must all novels end with an earthly marriage, and nothing be left for heaven?

Perhaps, for such as Hope, this life is given to show what happiness might be, and they await some other sphere for its fulfilment. The greater part of the human race live out their mortal years without attaining more than a far-off glimpse of the very highest joy. Were this life all, its very happiness were sadness. If, as I doubt not, there be another sphere, then that which is unfulfilled in this must yet find completion, nothing omitted, nothing denied. And though a thousand oracles should pronounce this thought an idle dream, neither Hope nor I would believe them.

It was a radiant morning of last February when I walked across the low hills to the scene of the wreck. Leaving the road before reaching the Fort, I struck across the wild moss-country, full of boulders and footpaths and stunted cedars and sullen ponds. I crossed the height of land, where the ruined lookout stands like the remains of a Druidical temple, and then went down toward the ocean. Banks and ridges of snow lay here and there among the fields, and the white lines of distant capes seemed but drifts running seaward. The ocean was gloriously alive,—the blackest blue, with white caps on every wave; the shore was all snowy, and the gulls were flying back and forth in crowds; you could not tell whether they were the white waves coming ashore, or bits of snow going to sea. A single fragment of ship-timber, black with time and weeds, and crusty with barnacles, heaved to and fro in the edge of the surf, and two fishermen's children, a boy and girl, tilted upon it as it moved, clung with the semblance of terror to each other, and played at shipwreck.

The rocks were dark with moisture, steaming in the sun. Great sheets of ice, white masks of departing winter, clung to every projecting cliff, or slid with crash and shiver into the surge. Icicles dropped their slow and reverberating tears upon the rock where Emilia once lay breathless; and it seemed as if their cold, chaste drops were sent to cleanse from her memory each scarlet stain, and leave it virginal and pure.

CPSIA information can be obtained at www.ICGtesting.com
Printed in the USA
BVOW06s1525290715

410551BV00011B/40/P